T0304439

The Blue Light

THE ARAB LIST

Hussein Barghouthi

THE BLUE LIGHT

Translated by Fady Joudah

LONDON CALCUTTA NEW YORK

SERIES EDITOR
Hosam Aboul-Ela

Seagull Books, 2023

First published in Arabic as *a l-Daw' al-azraq*

© Petra Barghouthi and Athar Barghouthi, 2004, 2023

English translation © Fady Joudah, 2023

ISBN 978 1 80309 083 2

British Library Cataloguing-in-Publication Data
A catalogue record for this book is available from the British Library

Typeset by Seagull Books, Calcutta, India
Printed and bound in the USA by Integrated Books International

For Bari, Suzan, and Don,
these words about the blue light.

CHAPTER ONE

I met him: a Sufi from Konya, Turkey, of the order of whirling dervishes whose patron saint, our maula Jalal Edin Rumi, had prescribed dancing for them and himself. The Sufi from Konya said that his father was a Turkish military officer who had come to the United States on a military-exchange program, and that is how he got to grow up here. He studied philosophy and political psychology, then decided to research the laws that govern consciousness and the cosmos. He went back to Turkey, became a Sufi, and then abandoned everything, turned mad or homeless or any other explanation we ascribe to those we don't understand.

In those days, I was a master's student in comparative literature at the University of Washington, Seattle, or at least that's what I looked like I was. On the inside, I was on the edge of madness. I was terrified, possessed by the feeling that I was about to lose my mind. I had come to this city to flee from big cities like New York, because I didn't have time for New York or for the personalities of big cities. I was looking for an area with reasonable weather and some downtime to organize my chaos.

For months I talked to no one. I wandered alone at night in the woods that surrounded the campus, thinking, thinking, thinking . . . about something, within a context, in some poem or horizon, until I realized that the problem was not with what I thought but with how I thought. My mind was a camera whose lens was imprecise, unfocused, and dysfunctional . . . That lens was how I thought.

I'd been thinking it for a while: that I was going mad. Whenever I shaved my face, I'd stare into the mirror and speak to myself: "Stay the course."

During my childhood, I used to lose awareness every once in a while. In 1964, in Beirut, I went to Cinema Carmen to watch *Julius Caesar*. After the movie, I walked out into the streets, their lights, cars, and modern bustle, and suddenly didn't know where I was, how to get home, couldn't recognize the place or its people, and grew more scared when the rumors of child-kidnapping gangs crossed my mind. For example, a veiled woman on a bus at the Lebanese-Syrian border: it was summer, extreme heat, sweaty faces, and in her lap a wrapped infant. The police officer asked her to uncover the child's face lest the child die of asphyxiation. She refused. Suspicious, he removed the wrapping and found a dead child that traffickers had disemboweled and stuffed with hashish before they sowed it back up. This rumor merged in my mind with the movie I had just seen: Caesar's face on his deathbed, dripping sweat, full screen.

I didn't know where I was. I asked a man passing by in the crowd if I was on the right track to Corniche al-Mazra'a. He called to another man and entrusted me to him. I walked with that other man in streets that I had walked a thousand times before, yet they all seemed strange to me. I didn't recognize any of them. Usually I'd come out of this state that resembled hypnosis or somnambulism when I recognized something I knew, some sign that returned me to a familiar awareness.

Then God sent the sign: a florist shop near our house. I woke up and told the stranger man that our house is here. He tried to convince me that it couldn't be, that it was farther away. I refused. He took back the liras he had bribed me with and tried to drag me by my wrist. I was well built and he found it difficult to pull me. I spotted two cops by the entrance to the offices of the magazine *Hawadith*—a building with mosaic-blue balconies that I used to call "the blue building"— and pointed to the cops, threatened the man that I'd call them. That saved me.

"Losing awareness?" A peculiar case, undefined, on repeat.

By 1985, my condition had worsened. I resorted to sleeping pills and pills for my nerves. I was asleep at our house one night when I felt something like a kiss on my eyes and I snapped straight up and frightened.

I shook so intensely I could sense every artery in my body, every nerve, a surge of extraordinary energy. I was dancing like a doll, unable to hold a natural posture, felt like I was about to die right then and there, in two seconds, from a heart or brain explosion, and started running so that I may squander some of that energy. It was 1 a.m., and I ran and ran with all my strength for almost an hour. When I stopped, I found myself in deserted mountains, in the wild, away from human and jinn. The moon disc was close by and over my head. White clouds were swimming around it. The moon was about to fall on me. A séance of sorts. As if the universe was about to swallow me whole. I slapped my forehead and muttered to myself: "This is a moon, don't forget! This is *the* moon, don't forget!"

All that which I called "mind," all the "names" of things, and all my "memory" appeared in the back of my head, like a useless portfolio. And then a new presence emerged, as if God had transfigured.

I remained in that state until sunrise. By first light I leaned on a rock and passed out, asleep and exhausted. I felt safe, so safe, when night ended.

Introduction to the Psychology of Fog:

Strange how place appears as a ruse sometimes. For a reason mysterious to me, I spent most of my time in Seattle frequenting three places: Grand Illusion Cinema, Blue Moon Tavern, and Last Exit Café.

Their names attracted me. Blue Moon most especially. Particularly the color.

It is said that blue is an antidote to sexual excitation—and I was a raging bull then. It is also said that blue calms the nerves—and I was on the edge of madness, bad temper was my inheritance, my father was known for it.

I said the color drew me in. The Naqshbandi Sufi order believes that within each human there are multiple selves and that to each self there's a light, an illumination specific to it. Blue is the color of the sinful self, the one that commands bad deeds. (Not only did my self command me to wrongdoing, but also to crime, and I was concerned that I would split in two: one self that commits a crime, and one that doesn't know about it.)

Red is the color of the inspired self. White is the color of the serene self. Green the color of the self that is content with itself. Black is of the self that God has contented. And yellow is for the judgmental self.

Still, in my opinion, each self has its private set of colors. In Tibetan Buddhism, they say that blue is the color of the first being that has overflowed our colorless and formless first nature. Blue is the color of the energy of creation within us. I remember how years ago I would shut my eyes and listen to Stravinsky, Beethoven, or Mozart. I used to imagine myself in a wadi in the mountains of my childhood. And the wadi was a bewildering dark blue, the rocks were dark blue and magical. Was that an awareness of suppressed creative energy or a longing for childhood? Or was it total estrangement? I'm not sure, but my interest in blue is old, since I was a kid. The name of Zarqa' al-Yamamah, for example, was stuck in my mind. Just because her name was strange and blue, the blue woman of Yamamah. Only recently I reconsidered her name.

Zarqa' was the most famous oracle of pre-Islamic Arabs. She could see into distances no one else could. She would survey the landscape and warn her people of things to come. One day, she saw walking trees. Invaders had cut off tree branches, raised them over their heads and walked to evade her sight. No one believed her vision. The invaders reached Yamamah and destroyed it. They captured Zarqa' and sought to tear out her eyes, the secret of her powers. They found her eyes stuffed with black antimony, a stone that ancient Arabs crushed into powder for kohl, mascara that men and women wore. Zarqa' was the first to use it.

The black rocks were sacred to Ishtar, the lunar goddess. For that reason, kohl, as fine crystals of black antimony, was the equivalent of prayer to the moon goddess, so that she might inspire men and women toward far-sightedness, oracular vision, as was the case with Zarqa's eyes, stuffed with black antimony, because Zarqa' is a priestess of the moon. As for the story about the walking trees, it travelled west and became common in European literature. The Three Witches foretold Macbeth of his end. They said that when Dunsinane Forest walks, he dies.

But I wasn't satisfied that the myth of Zarqa' solved the riddle of her name. It is possible that blue is a divine color to bind both blues: sea and sky. Zoroastrian Persians believed that Ahura Mazda, the God of Wisdom, had a blue destructive enemy, Ahriman. Blue is satanic as well.

For me, blue is the color of estrangement, the unknown, and of the childhood sky. And maybe there is, also, blueness to my ill wishes. When I learned to play the piano, I composed a short magical piece, played it for a while, day after day, without knowing the secret of my love for it, until one day I read a book by a Black musician who claimed that each note has a color specific to it. And each composition, too. One of Mozart's sonatas arouses in the listener green or blue or . . . anyway, I looked for the color of that magical note of mine and was astonished to find it was blue. I recognized my special love of blues music, which has a note called the blue note: *His grandpa had an empire / his granny had an empire / and in the middle of Chicago, he got away with crime / and ran at night on the hills of San Fran howling like a wolf.*

For Black people in the United States, blue is the color of suffering: "What did I do to be so black and blue?" (I think Louis Armstrong said in a song).

As I said, the name Blue Moon stayed with me. When I went inside, I found the Tavern was old and dirty and faded, and that the city had tried to demolish it to construct a shopping center in its place. But a group of intellectuals rose up. For them, Blue Moon was a historic marker of Seattle's soul.

During the Sixties, when the revolutionary movement erupted and shook the United States—the Civil Rights and anti-Vietnam war movements—many of the figures and symbols of those movements passed through the Tavern. Blue Moon is a dense revolutionary memory.

In Seattle, there was a lot of longing for those Sixties. But between the blue in the Tavern's name and the current reality, there was an abyss that looked like a lie. A wooden shelf across the Tavern's walls was stacked with old books. Countless cigarette butts on the patio. Drunks and hippies at the tables. And an old pool table whose blue felt was peeling off.

Last Exit Café had a pallid wall color. Its wallpaper had succumbed to the appetite of time. On those walls, anyone who thought they were an artist hung their terrible work. I asked the owner once about the criteria for hanging up a painting, and he said: "No criteria. Only one condition: the painting must not be worse than the wallpaper."

Last Exit had a different color, especially at night: vulgar wooden tables, and on each table a sallow-red kerosene lamp. The place was haunting, ghostly, leaning to yellow.

When I was a child, our village in Palestine had no electricity. I used to read and write to the light of a kerosene lamp. This is why lamp colors reside in the deep valleys of my unconscious. Secretly, I felt that the yellow-red ghostly light in Last Exit bound me to my childhood.

I don't know what the form of this yellow region in my soul is. A painter once told me that yellow is the color of fear. The Naqshbandi Sufis were right, at least as it relates to my condition: yellow is the color of guilt. Truth is, I was under

8

the spell of the yellow lights of Ramallah's streets. They used to baffle me just as they baffled the American professor who taught philosophy in Birzeit University. He used to sit on his balcony at night with one lit candle and a bottle of wine, a ritual that eventually led to losing his sight. I'd spot him standing for hours at the entrance of his apartment building in Ramallah, staring at the yellow streetlights. Yellow is my feeling of guilt and fear. The Ramallah night is a liquid black painting. A yellow canal runs through it.

White is arid. In Palestine, noon is totally white. In sunlight, everything is clear, precise, lacks suggestion. In white, I create nothing. I need some kind of mystery for my creative forces to wake up. A lunar color, for example, as when mountains overflow with shadows, and the boundaries of objects melt. A cypress tree by the cemetery becomes a woman in a black aba, like my mother, who tries to embrace me.

I was quite young when a brother of mine died in the Sixties. Back then, they used to bury children in one of the Roman caves they called Pistachio because its dirt was pistachio color. They buried my brother in Pistachio. My mother said that children don't die, they become green birds in a paradise with flowing rivers. I wasn't convinced. On an empty, spacious and moonlit night, I went to Pistachio. I wanted to get my brother out of there. I imagined all of the children coming out in white shrouds—if they were even shrouded—and flowing in moonlight before they began to walk in gardens, in the shade of olive trees, in silence. Moon color is evidence of the wakeful power of the imagination that refashions the world to what is feminine within us—evidence of the "White Goddess" who made Zarqa' al-Yamamah wear a kohl of crystal powder out of black rock.

In Palestine, the color of memory is lunar. The moon is the only nightlight that clarifies to the peasants the features of objects. The other light was of lanterns that illuminate the graves of holy saints.

And for a Palestinian villager like me, it's hard to understand estrangement—whether from home or from self— without understanding the transfer of Palestinian culture in the twentieth century from light to light: from the moon lantern to electricity and neon . . . white neon like stomach acid, unbearable and cold, an electric sun bent on destroying the brain.

Strange how place seems like a ruse, sometimes. I found myself wandering these three joints looking for myself, not among books, I was sick of books, but among the shady and the crazy, the homosexuals and punks, where maps are clearer, more precise, and more exciting, or where at least I, as one of them, didn't have to talk to anyone. For a whole nine months, I talked to no one. I knew no one. I used to walk until morning in the woods that surrounded the university. Still, God surrounded me with the marginal world and all its gravitational pull.

On a trail within the surrounding woods I saw a guy, his beard was down to his waist. It was totally white, and his face, the flushed rose of alcohol. He was smiling to me with such joy as if he were seeing a human for the first time. He was an extremely happy man who sat on a stone step with a bottle of Vodka and asked me for two dollars: "Who are you?" he said. "I am Hussein. My name is Hussein. And you?" "I am God," he said. I laughed and asked, "What brings you to Earth?" He said, "I have a girlfriend in Seattle." Then he laughed again, innocently, "Welcome," he said.

Just around the corner from this guy who thought he was God was an electric toy store for those who think they are humans. All forms of violence that God or his creatures had created were in that metal-frame building: karate, racecars, regional bombardment, duels with ghosts, air strikes. I used to sit inside the store and watch its customers. I noticed one particular person who regularly came around midnight in Marines' attire, military gloves and boots. He would perform all the rituals of flying, then sit down and play his game with utmost seriousness: his offensive on The Red World, or The Evil Empire as Ronald Reagan had called the Communists. Each person here was possessed by an imaginary idea of themselves. The idea that he was a pilot, for example, or a superior Kung Fu player in an ancient Chinese temple . . . or other ideas: as when a Black man came up to me looking for trouble because my hair was long and blond, and it was that that bothered him. He touched my hair with disdain and said it was pretty.

Each one of us fights their private ghosts. And he was a young man possessed by an old White ghost, since the days of White people hunting Black people in Africa to sell them in "The New World." I said to him or to the ghost in him: "I am not from America and I am not White. I am from Palestine." He stopped mocking me and left. His problem was Whiteness in the world. He had a friend with a big belly, a nose like a mushroom, a slant smile and, all in all, ugly. When he found out I was an Arab, he sat next to me and told me that Arabs are not from Africa, they were colonizers who invaded it and settled it in the north, and that they should leave the continent. He was an African nationalist, he said. I said I was Palestinian, and I've not been to Africa, not even the Arab part of it. Not many Black people came to this big White store. Those who did became consumed with their Blackness.

Once, I said to a beautiful Black woman outside the store, a director of a documentary film I did not see, that we Arabs feel a disturbance in the depths of our identities and look for our roots in Islam in the seventh century or farther back. Some go back to their Pharaonic or Phoenician or Cretan roots. For example, we Palestinians come, as they say, from Sea Peoples that used to roam the Mediterranean, and some of us come from Crete, thousands of years ago. No matter how old they are, these roots are live roots. Imagine how PLO fighters, after they were forced out of Beirut on ships in 1982, returned to their origins: the sea. When their ships reached Crete, the Cretans received them on the shore and served them feast after feast and told them "You are our prodigal children."

She said "The problem for Black people is different. If we try to return to 'our beginning' in America, we return to slavery in cotton fields, and you just can't build an identity whose foundation is being a slave in one's eyes and in the eyes of others."

Maybe that was what led Malcolm X in prison to the notion that God is Black, as he wrote in his memoirs. Identity is colored.

The next day, she was nowhere to be found. I never saw her after that. In this world of the margin, everyone transits as through a scene in a movie. In the crowd, there are geniuses and mind destroyers and those in-between . . . like Johnnie.

Johnnie had a broken set of upper teeth. Only the front upper two remained so that he looked like a rabbit, long and thin, always donning a kind smile. I asked him about himself, and he said that his mom had been murdered: "Little green men killed her, they came from Deep Space." "Which part?" I asked. "Near Green Lake." "How can you be so sure? Maybe her killers are from Planet Earth," I added. He clarified: "The American government caught them, and they confessed." "And what will the American government do with them? Will they also apply US laws to residents of Deep Space?" "No," he said, "they will send to every victim like myself a little green man to do with what we want." "And what will you do with a man from Deep Space who was mail-delivered to you from D.C.?" He smiled his usual smile and expressed his admiration of my front teeth, then said: "I will send him to school in Seattle, to show him that we have excellent schools, just as they do up there."

Johnnie disappeared for two months, then popped up wearing a cowboy hat at the front of the toy store, still smiling. "What happened?" I asked. "Nothing. I was walking naked in the street and the cops arrested me without cause. They're crazy." He was shaking his head in wonder at their behavior.

Johnnie used to sleep in particular spots, by a tree trunk, for example, and sometimes other homeless men usurped his place. That's Johnnie, a man without place who has forged for himself an imaginary identity, a narrative of the loss of his mother, her link to green creatures from Deep Space.

Occasionally, under the influence of drugs, he would imagine that dinosaurs were looking at him from treetops. He lived profoundly in his imagination . . . and yet, who am I? A person who insists that he has a "real" identity? Why don't I sculpt a story, from the top of my head about my "roots"? What's the proof that my roots are real?

Johnnie is a levitational, airy being who bears no history. As for those among us who are born under the Mediterranean sign (as I was), we are the inheritors of the Agrarian Revolution, the domestication of cattle in the Stone Age, and the founding of small towns and cities. We are the inheritors of the oldest revolution in human history. And this bottomless history has impersonated or possessed me: I was born in a village and my memory is the memory of a village. Egypt and Babylon are my heritage. But the likes of Johnnie have no memory except that of modern big cities. He's never heard of a village or peasants. White American civilization, like Johnnie, has a lightweight unmentionable history. In the Mediterranean, history is deep and heavy. In America, it's superficial and, to an extent, shallow. Encountering Johnnie, I felt that I came from another universe, from a tunnel that stretches back to the Stone Age. I am not the wholesome son of modern big cities.

Johnnie had a German friend, gay and gentle, with a shaved head and a red bandana, a smart guy. At the electric-toy store, he said, "This is a place that sells sex and fantasy." Precise. Few capture the notion of this "Fantasy Industry." As for the world of the margin in which he exists, he said, "Its edges are anxious." "What edges?" "The edges on both sides of the fence that separate the ordinary folks from the homeless ones!" "The fence": I liked the expression.

Strange, how place becomes a ruse. I was sane, educated, intellectual, a graduate student, and everything seemed all right, while inside me there was a desert in which a creature knelt amid the emptiness, "eating his heart out," as some English poet said. I asked that creature about the taste: "Is it bitter?" "Very bitter, my friend," he said.

Grand Illusion Cinema mocked me. All of my life was a tiny illusion, that much I knew. But the possibility that my life was a grand illusion was new to me: a small cafe with small steps, and on the roof, a canopy that changed, with time and rain, into an ashen gloomy mixture of green and blue. Under the canopy, wooden chairs that looked even gloomier and older. It was there, on one such seat, from where I could see the rain fall like relentless prison bars around me, that I met Suzan. She was the wreckage of a woman from the Sixties' revolution, ill looking, with a ripe face and wide, desirous red lips. Her face, wrapped in a white handkerchief, blushed like that of a young girl's, and if she moved her face, her fat glands in her chin jiggled along. She had no lover, no mother, no father, no friend. All she owned was a white notebook for sketching a blue peacock. Always a blue peacock.

She was sitting on her chair and staring at me when she spoke: "You live inside your head." The accuracy of the phrase shocked me. "I live in my head" means that I am not even half-alive, that there is a desert or a corpse inside me, one and the same. On the exterior, I was jovial, confident, full of vigor, pretending to be. And I was not sure how to separate a person from what they pretend to be or claim they are.

I invited her to the house. My place had a glass wall inside. On the bookshelf that swallowed the other half of the wall was a pine branch I had found during one of my nocturnal strolls in the woods. She laughed satirically, "A pine branch among books?" I laughed back and said, "There's life in it." She shook her head as she took a drag from her cigarette and said, "Contradiction." I understood what she didn't say: if one is filled with life, then one doesn't need to bring a pine branch inside to spread in him a feeling of life.

She had no idea then about my fear of madness or of committing a crime. And I had no idea how terrified I was underneath all this appearance of sanity. When my friend, the Palestinian filmmaker Sobhi Zobeidi, visited me in Seattle, he spoke to me of his New York lawyer friend. He said: she is certain she's crazy, and her proof is that she thinks she's sane. The mind, then, is a safety valve in the face of some invisible internal terror. What's the difference between me and her, the lawyer? Nothing. I am scared of madness as I grip reason. She is sane and clutches madness. And both of us want to survive an invisible thing.

As I said, I was searching for a solution in the marginal world, this world of Johnnie and Suzan . . . and I ended up with a Church. Was my perception unjust to this Church or was the Church as I had seen it? My condition didn't allow me a clear understanding of things. This is my story with the Church.

On University Avenue, I passed by a door to a building where two young women stood handing out pamphlets. Two white faces, the kind that distinguishes the American middle class: nothing disturbs or muddies it. Two neutrally beautiful faces that don't bear a shy blush or a yellow fear or desire. Two faces that also reminded me of the Sphinx: generations were wiped out, but nothing changed it or its face. I couldn't walk too far past them. I considered myself an expert in reading faces and since I didn't understand what I had just seen, I went back to them.

They said they belonged to the Church of Dianetics. We went inside and up the stairs. On the first floor was a woman who possessed neutral white beauty, a replica of the two young women. She sat in front of two empty cans connected via wires to a primitive electrical device. She asked me to grab the two cans, a hand on each, as I answered her questions, and that through the aid of this device she would map out "the destruction" in my life. That word "destruction" got my attention. It's an allegation, an intelligent suggestion that I am not only "destroyed" but that I also don't understand my "destruction" unless this small tin can attempts to save me. The whole matter started as a joke, but when I looked at myself I saw "certain damage": a fear of madness, let's say, an anxiety. Then I thought to myself: the woman is nothing but "a small person," as Wilhelm Reich put it: "a person who knows your weak points, my little one, and takes advantage of them, is a small person, just as you are." Her words manipulated my weakness, my fear of madness, my anxiety and trepidation about identity—and who doesn't possess fears that can't be manipulated?

With my right hand on the left can, my left on the right, she started asking me about me, and at the end of the session she handed me my "destruction" map, a "detailed destruction" that leads to the next obvious step. The Church would save me from my ruin with the aid of a can. "And how much does salvation cost?" I asked. "There are courses that cost upwards of fifty thousand dollars," she replied. And when I laughed at the enormity of the amount, she added "You can enroll in a course for about fifty dollars." I wrote her a check. She sent me to another desk. Behind it sat a wheat-colored man with deep cracks in his face, the remains of some old illness, but his face was calm, also neutral, wearing the same veil that the other faces were wearing. He spoke: "Our Church attracts the more sensitive and intelligent minds." At the first desk I was "destroyed," and at the second desk I became smart and sensitive—allegations of destruction are followed by praise to pump the customers full of hot air. To get to the bottom of this neutrality that pervaded all the faces in this building, as if I were in a laboratory with proliferating clones, I decided to provoke him: "I already bargained with the woman at the entrance on the price of salvation."

My accusation that the Church turns people's vulnerabilities into transactions did the trick. A muscle on the right corner of his mouth swelled blue, unconsciously quivered, as if a repressed rage three thousand years old trembled inside, as if one lonely, isolated spot in his facial meta-serenity had been forever disfigured. If you focused your attention on just this spot, you'd see a face that recalls what Nizar Qabbani wrote:

> Together we tumbled to the bottom, two trains
> of fractures and shards, fully disfigured
> like found creatures from prehistoric times.

"Brainwashing" occurred to me: this serenity on these faces is not beauty but the calm of the brainwashed. I'm not going to lie: I felt a kind of horror that I might become a doll in the hands of some representative who controls me from a distance through a device. But I decided to gamble and signed up for a course.

The course was held in a spacious, well-organized hall. First lesson: a young trainer in his late twenties, with a washed-away face like the others, spoke in a monotonous ordinary voice interrupted by measured pauses between sentences. He grabbed a tennis ball, tossed it to me, and instructed me to return it to him, so I tossed it back.

"This is called human communication. Speech is like the ball, when you don't return it, play is disrupted." A valuable exercise that suggests I was a kid in first grade.

Second lesson: sit in your chair and close your eyes. "Don't think of anything, just be here, hear all the sounds outside you, and relax." Another helpful exercise. I spent four hours with my eyes closed listening to the outside. Other lessons followed daily. There was no room for personal chats with the trainer who seemed to perform a task that didn't concern him. But after many sessions and trials I got him to talk. I asked him: When was he born? His answer amazed me: "I was born five thousand years ago in Babylon. My soul moved from one body to the next until it settled in me here and now." This was no innocent belief in incarnation, this was brainwashing. They changed his very identity. He was no longer from Seattle, for example, but Babylonian, beyond death, beyond time and place, unsusceptible to endings. Later he explained his belief that time was made up of cycles, that each cycle might last for centuries, and that at the end of each cycle he'd die and then be recreated into the next cycle. It was clear: this was identity erasure. At the end of this cycle, some big shot representative of the Church would tell him that his current time was up, that he'd need to commit suicide or die in some manner they'd determine for him, so that he could be reborn in the upcoming sequence. And if his saviors felt like he knew too much, they might finish him off sooner with just two words: "Time's up." He'd willingly kill himself.

Perhaps they would have erased my ancient identity, reassembled it to give birth to me "in the fourth century BCE" in Babylon, Nineveh, or Athens. Do certain intelligence agencies fund these brainwashing experiments? Whatever it was, I felt terrified that I would lose my mind as I'd never feared before. I left the Church, but for a long while it wouldn't leave me. It hounded me with pamphlets, with its founder Hubbard's books, and with members who wanted to meet with me until I was fed up with my soul. Sometimes kindness to people is a crime against self.

It seemed that a kind of fate was always directing my foot-steps to places that turn out to be a ruse—wrong places—and I began to feel that my life was simply a series of deviations from "the real Hussein," the life I was meant to live but con-stantly evaded my grip. So, I kept on with my all-nighter strolls in the woods on campus, thinking, thinking, thinking. One evening, on the high treetops, tens of black birds let out dreadful cries before they descended on me as a predator might, their wings so close to my face that I had to swing at them with my arms. I felt absurd, as if I were in a Hitchcock film.

It was after this incident that I met a friend of Suzan's who was worse than those birds. He had a firm body, a coarse face, chewed tobacco and spit it, and his attire was always the bright orange, yellow, and red of the Rajneesh disciples.

Rajneesh, an Indian man, came to the United States carrying a message of ecstasy, joy, enlightenment, and dancing. Behind this "guru," a cult formed and put on the colors of ecstasy, joy, enlightenment, and dancing. And as with the members of the Church of Dianetics, Rajneesh's disciples all looked alike: in ecstasy, joy, enlightenment, and dancing. Suzan's friend, the version of Rajneesh in Seattle, composed trash poetry stuffed with joy, ecstasy, enlightenment, and dancing. His secret lay in his absolute selfishness, an individualist with a narrow horizon, angry, without joy, ecstasy, enlightenment, or dancing. His existence was more fraudulent than mine. He was a drug addict. We were roommates for no more than two days before I kicked him out.

I used to live in a studio apartment. In the middle of it, he hung an orange-yellow-red cloth with dirty stains that emitted the scent of Indian incense and spice, so that joy, ecstasy, enlightenment, and dancing might permeate his soul. He then prohibited me from passing through his curtain to anywhere. There are those who are afflicted with cosmic constipation and poetic diarrhea and don't know that the problem of their poetry is not in their poetry but in their ruined relations with the universe and life—that no "Rajneesh" can change them or their poetry unless they change themselves first. My roommate dated a lost young woman from Chicago, a runaway. She was as shaky as a tennis net and moved in with us. She told him that he was gay, disinterested in sex with her. He took it to mean that she had a thing for me, and since I didn't feel joy, ecstasy, enlightenment, or dancing, and was not a member of his sect, he physically attacked me, so I kicked him out.

In Grand Illusion, we met all sorts of people like this. Suzan told me once while staring at the rain falling down like prison bars, "We are not of flesh and blood, we came from story and to story we go. Write a story about us, Hussein. We're a story."

No story of mine would be complete without Don. A homeless painter with a light red beard and a small bald spot on his head that he covered with a gray beret. A transparent, fragile being, gentler than a shed tear. Before he spoke, he'd form a semicircle with his beard on his chest, in slow motion, like he was overcoming a repressed force that would otherwise prevent him from speech. And when he spoke his voice was like a prayer.

I still remember him standing there, playing pool in Blue Moon Tavern, next to that Sufi from Konya who stretched his neck toward Don and said: "I've got nothing to do with others." And Don replied: "Go be a jellyfish then." And the Sufi rolled a cigarette while muttering: "Oh, God is talking."

That night, Don came to my studio apartment. His beard was dripping rain. He was a mess, and he held a filthy, wet wooden ring. I thought he needed a place to sleep so I invited him in. He handed me the wooden ring instead.

—This is a gift for you. I found it in the trash.

—What is it, Don?

—Take it. It's the mind. A circle of three hundred and sixty degrees, and within each degree there are infinite degrees.

—Yes, infinite degrees, Don, but what does it have to do with the mind?

—Each degree has its manner of looking into life and living. Learn from this wooden ring to see in circles, in three hundred and sixty degrees, sit in the empty center and look fully around you, and stay in the empty center.

He disappeared into the dark rain to sleep on the streets. And I stayed standing with wind and ring. I washed the ring and hung it on the wall. The mind is a wheel. Whenever the wheel turns, our way of seeing ourselves, life, and living changes. And we change.

On a following morning, Don asked to come with me to campus. "No, Don, come on, the last thing I need is some trouble at the university. You can join me on one condition: that I enter the hall through one door, you through another, so that no one thinks we're together." He rubbed his red beard in a circle over his chest like he was kneading hard clay, "Fine, Hussein, that's fine. I enter through one door, you through another."

The professor was Yugoslavian. She belonged to the old aristocracy that Tito had destroyed after establishing his Communism in Yugoslavia. In the lecture hall, she spoke with her nose in the air, her head high as if she was dancing flamenco, still inhabiting the same inherited aristocratic positions. The lecture was about World Literature. "The first person to use the expression 'World Literature' was Goethe," she said. "Then Marx and Engels observed in the *Communist Manifesto* that various national literatures of different peoples had started to form a World Literature." Don raised his arm suddenly. The entire hall turned toward him, all eyes shifted and took notice. "Did you know that ancient Greek statues used to see? The Greeks used to paint the statues' eyes and lashes. The statues had eyes and could see as people could, they weren't blind as you might think." The professor didn't know what was going on. Bewildered, she replied: "No, I didn't know they could see." "You didn't know?" Don spoke. "Well, go be a jellyfish then." And gathered his thin, delicate stature out of the hall.

Some time passed before I saw Don again. I thought he didn't want to see me any more until one morning I was surprised to see him standing by a stone fence, spreading some trash over it, an empty rusty Coke can, bits of paper. He was organizing and reorganizing his "furniture." "Hello, Don." He looked at me. His face was hungry, his hair blown, his eyes held a fugitive expression. He wasn't fully aware. "Hello, Don, this is me, Hussein." "Hussein? Who's Hussein?" he asked with a low soft voice, then disappeared briefly in thought as if he were trying to remember: "Hussein! I don't know anyone by that name." He laughed at my strange appearance and returned to organizing his trash.

Don used to lose his awareness now and again, long or short term, during which he'd recognize no one. I used to lose my awareness, too, but with lesser intensity and greater brevity than he did.

Anyhow, when he regained his awareness, he recognized me again, and I didn't mention the episode to him or what had transpired in the lecture hall. I just complained to him about my boredom with Seattle. "Let's change the scenery," he said and invited me to a bus station. We rode to another town on the coast then boarded a ferry for a long while into the blue waves, the sun, the foam, and air. We reached a small island with a small forest. A divine sight. The breadth of the blue ocean undisturbed, except for a ghetto, a reservation of Indigenous Americans opposite a US naval base, the victim and victimizer in one swoop. On the lip of a steep rocky slope that resembled a chasm (I am afraid of heights) stood a beautiful wooden lodge. Don went straight to it, took a key chain out of his pocket, and entered. A spacious living room, beautiful furniture, kitchen, library. "Come in, this is my house!" I was stunned: "Don, you paint in the streets and this is your house? Paint here!" "Take the keys and live in it yourself," he said. I stood silent. "You're like my mother, you don't get the soul of an artist." And he pointed through the window to another house, the only other one on the island, also on the edge of a cliff. "That is the house of one of the Masonic leaders. The regime in the US is Masonic." "How?" "Look at the dollar bill," he said, "it contains the Great Pyramid and the Eye of Horus, a well-known Masonic symbol." I kept quiet. But I realized later that what he said was historically correct. "We will spend the night here." "Here?" "Yes, the ferry doesn't cross back today."

Oh God, I tried to imagine the night there alone, in the forest, on the island, by the ocean's rumble, a prologue to losing my mind. The energy of the place was strong, it reminded me of a mountain I visited in Snoqualmie. A falls tumbling through the groove of the mountain between humidity and black stone. I climbed for hours until sunset and I still had hours to go before I reached the peak. I pulled out a piece of bread, but a bird landed on my hand and started pecking at my food but in peace, only as a bird that doesn't know humans well might. Back in Palestine, the birds are hysterical. They evade any sign that points to a bond between them and humans, but that's another story. As I stood by the falls, the energy of the place at night saturated me with the feeling that to stay for one night within the vessel of this mountain would compel me to pray to forces I know nothing about.

In Don's house I sat on a leather chair in the library and asked him about his obsession with trash. "Someone has to remove it," he said, "I or another." I wasn't convinced. He didn't sweep the streets. He selectively rummaged through trash: Coke cans, torn books, a damp wooden ring, dried leaves. Suzan knew this. She loved Don, tried to persuade him to abandon his hobby. "What else will I do with my life?" he told her. "That's a point, Don, you have a point, a point that has no answer," Suzan said. Sometimes history leaves people with nothing to do about their history.

It was during those days that I met him, that Sufi from Konya. He said he was originally from Turkey before he became American: "Though now, I am nothing, thank God." The first time I saw him I was with Suzan at Grand Illusion. She was addicted to drawing a blue peacock, and I was watching the drizzle over the asphalt. He came up the steps toward us. His energy caught my eye. It resembled the earth and mushrooms. But his form was that of an ancient pastoral warrior: a well-knotted heavy military boot ready for an emergency, a green winter US naval poncho, and a rough wild wooden stick with a bracelet tied to it, completely out of context. He leaned his stick on a wooden chair and rolled his Osman tobacco, a Turkish brand. His fingers were white, soft, feminine, their tips stained with nicotine, like henna, but his hands were masculine and thick and covered with black hair, a contradiction. I mean you can't gather his details into one thing. His skin was the color of wheat, with the deep, stiff wrinkles of someone who's accustomed to living outdoors, and his mustache was black, rectangular, with shattered corners that invite no eyes to settle on them or on his wide lips that rose unconsciously toward his nose. The nose, huge and arched, dominated his face. His voice was sea deep, as free as a roar, and of a different madness.

Suzan introduced me to him: "Bari, his name is Bari."

"I wrote a short story, Suzan, and if I were you I'd love to hear it," he said as he laughed and searched his pocket for a tattered, wet piece of paper: "Earlier on my way home I ran into an old friend, a rabbit. I told him to come with me: I have a big present that befits you: a carrot." Bari burst into laughter, joyfully went on reading, then abruptly did a strange move that I would see him perform many times later: it looked like an apparition had showed itself to him, and he faltered, refocused his gaze on some point in his mind, rapidly and fearfully blinked several times, shook his head firmly but gently, more than once, as if his vision was scrambled, as if he couldn't even see the paper he was holding. The whole move lasted a few seconds before he continued with his laughter, as if nothing were the matter: "He jumped on my table and ate the carrot. We chatted for a bit, then he jumped off the table and left behind another pile of shit for me. 'You have no sense of shame, man? You do this to me?' I told the rabbit. 'Only take from life what you give it,' the rabbit said."

27

The word shit was abrasive to my "aesthetic mind." Strange how that word became a stain of yellow fog that dispersed in the air and in my body, and I lost him and Suzan for a minute, as if that utterance also controlled what I paid attention to and what I didn't.

When he grabbed his stick and walked away, I recovered my attention. After a couple of steps, he turned around and addressed Suzan: "Come by the house sometime." His invitation seemed sexual, or else why did he exclude me? Was Suzan a rabbit looking for another carrot? Embarrassed, her face flushed. "Come by sometime, I got coffee," he added. And we all broke into laughter. Then he was gone.

Suzan returned to drawing her blue peacock in an empty moonlit spot in the Tavern. Blueness took on another dimension, reflected in the contiguous zone. She moved her head to my direction without lifting her eyes and spoke: "Bari has more than what you might think." Little did I know that she had uttered a prophecy.

In his voice were sea depths and the echoes of a roar that reminded me of a night in which I walked barefoot on wet sand on the shores of Acca. I had snuck into Acca without a permit from the Israeli military and was afraid the police would arrest me for infiltration. Ahead of the sand around my feet, there were faint lights that came through a restaurant's windows that seemed committed to expose me. I escaped to a spot where I'd stare into some mysterious moonlit foam, currents that formed and collapsed in black waves, undertow that rose and disappeared and rose again. That's how I thought of Bari's mouth when he smiled, like that foam, which reminded me of another foam in another sea in another time.

In the Sixties of the last century in Beirut, my mother was told that the amniotic crust that persisted in my baby sister's hair would go away only if her hair was washed in the sea. We went, my mother, my sister, and I, to the Military Club Pool at nightfall. Darkness had descended, and the raging sea leaned to black. Waves crashed into the rocks and ricocheted cold, moonlit spume. We went down a steep sandy slope. Where rock began, my mother stood scared, hesitant, walked toward a shallow pool, squatted, scooped up seawater in her hands and started washing my sister's hair. I squatted next to my mom, my back to the sea, fully occupied with catching a small leaping fish whose destiny had cornered it into an isolated channel. Suddenly my mom let out the scream of a terrorized animal. I felt a hand grab the back of my shirt at the same time as a wave submerged me to my waist. Mom's hand pulled me out of the sea, dragged me to the sandy slope. When it was clear that I was safe, she turned her attention to calm my crying sister. I felt fear in my legs and could barely climb up the incline to dry land. I looked back and the sea looked in the mood for a chase.

That night I dreamt that the sea was chasing me. For years the dream recurred. Mom advised me to place a page from the Quran under my pillow to "dispel evil." I chose the Maryam Surah, then the Yusef Surah, then the whole Quran, but the sea wouldn't relent.

I'd only seen the sea once in Beirut before that incident. It was during the summer. The sea's vastness, blueness, recurrence mesmerized me. I didn't get near it. I was the gruff son of mountains and I possessed the mountain's fear of the sea. I stood far back on the beach and took my clothes completely off, sat on a rock, my clothes in hand, and stared. It was the burning noon sun on glistening white sands, mirrors at boiling point. Seized by dry land's weariness of water, I observed the sea from a distance.

As I said, I'd dream the nightmare of the sea as it gave chase to me, not by the Military Club Pool where I almost drowned, but starting with my seated position on the rock on the beach, naked, with my clothes in hand. In the nightmare, the blueness gradually rises, the sea invites me to it, I take one step back, the sea rages, I take another step back, it persists. Then Beirut drowns in foam, roar, and crashing blue, street by street, and buildings implode, wood floats, people drown, and in the middle of the destruction, a gigantic monster, a King Kong I'd seen in Cinema Carmen, pulverizes buildings like cardboard boxes with his feet, while Mom's writhing in his hand as he holds her from her waist, raises her to the blue sky, but she doesn't escape, and I turn around, flee, not to the mountains in Aley or to the Cedar peaks of Lebanon, but to my childhood mountains in Ramallah: the nightmare always ends there—with me standing on the highest mountain around Ramallah, since around me all the other mountains have drowned—not a single mountain in the horizon, no horizon to speak of, only murky waters that float wood debris, dead birds, corpses, and the sea is calm, without Noah's dove or an olive branch, without terra firma in sight: I'm the only survivor, and the sea must wait for me to come down to it, the sea must not come up to me. The distance between us remains fixed. And when the next dream comes, the sea has receded to its original place, and I to mine. I am back on my rock, the blueness gradually rises, the dream repeats in endless circles.

My dad used to fear two things in Beirut: the sea and the cinema. At night, I'd wait until he was asleep, then through my room's window I'd leap out into a tiled courtyard with a glass door, and through that door I'd get to a corridor decorated with geometric gypsum and flower designs, Italian-style, then down the black and white marble stairs before breaking into a run through the back streets to Cinema Carmen. The show began nightly at 10 p.m. and ended at 1 a.m., three hours later. I was always the first person in the hall, to observe the guests, the seats filling up and, more important than the film itself, the drawing of the curtains to reveal an empty magical screen which emitted a dim light. I wanted so much to touch that magical screen. It couldn't be normal. What normal material could enable me to see Julius Caesar?

At the cinema's entrance, a Shiite fortune teller in black dress sat behind a wooden box on which sat two Indian rabbits: one was black, "bad omen," the other white, "good omen." An opening in the surface of the box was filled with folded paper scraps that had my luck written on them. She'd grab one rabbit by the scruff of the neck as if choking it, hover it over the opening, and when she released her grip, the rabbit would bite one of the scraps. She'd hand me my luck. I visited her often.

One luckless night, my dad woke up and didn't find me at home, found my window open and bed empty. He thought I was kidnapped by one of those gangs that disappear children, and he lost his mind.

At the cinema in Seattle's Grand Illusion, Bari's rabbit story reminded me of all that. The conclusion to that story, however, I'll make up: Dad came during the movie, asked the fortune teller if she'd seen a blond boy about ten years old enter the hall.

—A little boy? The fortune teller asked.

—Yes, ma'am, a little boy of the mountains who has nightmares about the sea, have you seen him?

—A mountain boy possessed by the sea?

—Yes, ma'am.

—It's all good. Your boy will travel far, very far, at sea, and he will look for two Indian rabbits and a box of paper scraps that will tell of his fortune, and he will return. It's all good, sir, a good omen.

His laughter, that Sufi from Konya, woke up the sea. Though his story of the rabbit awakened not only the fortune teller and her two rabbits, but also the memory of another rabbit.

In the Seventies of the last century, I worked at the Union of Engineers in Jordan. My workmate was a religious, obese man with a broad face and a meticulously trimmed beard. He was afflicted with the bug of grandiosity. He believed that he was the one responsible for bringing Khomeini to power in Tehran and would be the one to remove Sadat from power in Cairo. We used to call him "Your Excellence." Most amusing about His Excellence was his constant mention of a private rabbit. One time His Excellence was mumbling to himself, "The moon has resigned from love." "Whose love?" I asked. "The love of good folks," he said. "And who's the moon?" "The moon that loves the rabbit." "Which rabbit? There are many rabbits," I said. "The rabbit that lives up the mountain and every night sends big boulders rolling down to the wadi by my house, and my house, Mr. Hussein, is at the foothills."

We became friends because I respected his rabbit and he respected my professional skills. A little later the Iraqi regime executed a Jordanian student in Baghdad on the charges of espionage, and a diplomatic crisis erupted between the two countries. I commented on the matter impishly or banally, I'm not sure: "Did they execute the rabbit?" His Excellency's face quickly turned dark blue, cyanotic, and he rolled up his sleeves, walked over to my desk: "You're a stupid donkey, Mr. Hussein. You speak disrespectfully of those who are older than your father." "I am sorry Your Excellency, I am really sorry," I replied. Two days later I asked him, "How was the rabbit last night?" "He was quiet, didn't roll any boulders." And our friendship resumed.

Yes, it's true, I wasn't concerned at all with Bari or his world, didn't even register it as a world to begin with, but a particular incident tipped the balance.

I used to be a good chess player, played a lot, became a gambler. Some people, as I am, get hooked on whatever comes across their path: smoking, sex, chess, alcohol, collecting garbage, writing poetry, meeting a Sufi, etc. A person like that lives in series, from one fixation to another. That's what I used to do, exit one addiction to enter another. I lost my love for chess in the Seventies of the last century. Whether I won or lost a game, I felt nothing. So when I nonchalantly played Bari, and he beat me on the first couple of rounds, he broke into a guffaw, admiring himself and mocking me. For the third round, I concentrated and crushed him fast. He put his right hand under his belly, pushed it up, and muttered a weird prayer, a charm: "Pure Bari Om Mani Padme Hum" or something like that.

"Is something wrong?" I asked him. "They are," he said. "Who are they?" "Those who feed off my strength," he said. His language was magical but with a whiff of madness, or as Shakespeare said, "Though this be madness, there's a method in it." In the fourth round, I kept my concentration, intent on watching him lose. He performed that same mysterious move I'd seen him pull at Grand Illusion when he was reading his rabbit story: he stared off at some station in his fancy, scared as if he'd seen a ghost, dropped his head back as if he were distancing himself from a danger, blinked his eyes shut a couple of times, shook his head as if he were swatting a mosquito, and let out a laugh.

—What are you laughing about?

—Man, he said, there are more joyful creatures inside than outside.

I felt as if he were a red snail in the coiled shell of an expanding puzzle. When he lost the fourth game, he took a pencil I was holding and drew a circle in my notebook, redrew the circle again and again until I saw only one leaden spot, then he mumbled: "Pure Bari Om Mani Padme Hum." Suzan's words flashed through my mind: "There's more to Bari than meets your eye."

At Last Exit, they used to think he was another crazy person, schizophrenic perhaps like the majority of the clients there. I am not sure, though, why I sensed his madness was something more than the usual madness. His world drew me to it. Whenever we played chess at Last Exit, there'd be a very tall man who'd sit close to us. His name was Wayne. He buttoned his shirt all the way up, his neck stuck out like a duck's. His face wore a permeant stunned expression. And this

34

Wayne used to think I was a genius. He'd shut his eyes and focus whenever I spoke. I suggested that he concentrate another way, by opening his eyes, for example. And whenever he saw one of Bari's strange moves or heard Bari speak, he'd raise his eyebrows and say to me, "A hopeless space case."

For quite some time, whenever I asked Bari a question, he'd answer in a manner that reflected his disinterest in creating an opening or a portal for a real conversation. He rarely talked about his memories. I knew nothing about his past. He was a seaman, a cook, a Sufi, a college student, and homeless. That's all I knew. Like the sea, his world confused me. In it I sat, a child on a rock in the sand, naked, as I was in Beirut, staring at the expanse of this new sea: the fathoms of this being. Some time elapsed with Bari and me at a fixed distance from each other. He didn't flow like a sea, and I didn't flee like a child of the mountains. We were on a stage, frozen in place.

Last Exit held a weekly art night that was the pilgrimage of whoever rode a wind or strode on earth—blondes who the California sun had splattered into bronze statues, a musician I used to see at night in the campus woods conducting an orchestra that wasn't there, an Alaskan salmon fisherman with a one-string instrument he never played but occasionally and sensitively plucked as he whispered, "Ah, good vibes, good vibes"—those kinds of pilgrims.

A round table in the middle of the cafe encouraged dialogue between these types of worlds. At this exact table sat a homeless old woman in long, filthy, buttonless jacket. Its pockets were stuffed with torn paper. She kept a set of Tarot cards (a Pharaonic game I first heard of in T. S. Eliot's *The*

Waste Land). Her nose was pointy like a needle, shrewd and cunning like a witch's nose. But none of us could understand a word she spoke unless we handed her a couple of bucks. Otherwise her language was wreckage.

I gave her two dollars and she read my fortune: "You're on a distant path but you will become a free bird." I tried to lure her into talking about herself: "Where are you now?" She wrote out one sentence the size of half a page without spaces between letters or words: "I am on the path number three hundred." How does language turn into shells? There she was, another red snail with wreckage for speech, a snail invisible to all. Each individual at Last Exit had their private dictionary, which explained the constant "misunderstanding" between the cafe's patrons.

Suddenly it hit me, a brilliant idea: to author a dictionary of Bari's language. I'd specify the meaning of each of his words so that I may understand his world, and he mine. Otherwise that "fence" the gay German spoke of would remain between us. For example, the word "rabbit" for Bari meant "an old friend he invited for a carrot," whereas for me it meant two Indian rabbits of a Shiite fortuneteller, and for "His Excellence" it meant a rabbit who lives at night in the mountain and rolls boulders down on his house. Due to this polyvalence of meaning, no one could understand another. Total misunderstanding. Same between me and Bari. Words meant something entirely different for him than they did for me. Language is gifted in its capacity toward misunderstanding. Yes, I thought of inventing a dictionary for his private world, a project akin to that of an American Scientist who wanted to teach English to a chimpanzee so that the latter creature may function as a translator between the scientist and the rest of the chimp world.

A singer started to sing and brought me back to my surroundings. All the homeless in the cafe became his choir: "Long live America." I looked toward the exit and there was Bari standing, spitting the tobacco of a cigarette he'd just rolled. Our eyes met. He came toward me, confrontational: "Man, your blue bird came to me last night. Stop him."

I had no idea who my blue bird was, but I improvised a reply: "He was in his cage." "Are you calling me a liar, man?" "No, he must have escaped without my knowledge. I will stop him." "Thank you, I appreciate it." Then he left. Suzan asked me about this blue bird. "You know as much as I do," I told her, "I'm clueless." She couldn't stop laughing.

I started working on the dictionary. His talk about my blue bird, for example. What did blue mean to him? I tried to link "blue" to the weird prayer he was fond of repeating: "Pure Bari Om Mani Padme Hum," but in vain.

I drowned in searches that knew no beginning or end of holy universal texts. I stumbled on a beautiful, ancient, and astonishing text, "The Dream of the Blue Stag," in an amusing collection whose editor included the *Communist Manifesto* as one of the sacred texts. I recalled that Bari had recounted a meeting with an Indigenous Chief who was carrying a huge rifle on horseback: "I asked him 'How can you claim you represent a cosmic consciousness when you are the head of a tribe?' The Chief pointed his rifle at me, so I leapt on the barrel's mouth, perched like a little sparrow and chirped, 'The bullet won't reach me now, answer my question.' " Bari described the Chief's face and it seemed to match another face in "The Dream of the Blue Stag." I stumbled on volumes and anthologies: *The Sacred Writings of Oriental Sages*, or *The Sacred Texts of the East*. Another strange and phenomenal Tibetan book was *The Necklace of Clear Understanding*, translated into English as *Mind in Buddhist Psychology*, which Bari had read deeply. I frequented libraries of secrets, delved into Nostradamus, *I Ching*, Lao Tzu and the seven pillars of Zen, Dan Millman's *Way of the Peaceful Warrior*, and that book by Castaneda, the one he likely fabricated about Indigenous Americans. And from all this I reached the Upanishads.

I wrote down my notes in a pocketbook I always carried. I began to decipher Bari's mysteries. For example, in the margins to his charm, which he repeated as much as Suzan repeated her peacock drawing, I put down the following:

1. Pure: an English word.
2. Bari: his name, abbreviated from the Turkish "Bariş," which he mutated into the Arabic echo of the word for "innocent" or another echo of one of God's ninety-nine names. Maybe he altered his name because he believed that a name has magical power over the named, whether the latter is of stone or flesh. But that doesn't mean he wanted to alter his identity under the dominion of the new name. If "Bari" is derived from God's name, then Bari wants to resemble God, in the manner of Sufi similitudes as mentioned by Ibn Tufail in his book Hayy bin Yaqdhan. Bari's transcendent example is to become alive, alert, pure, and perhaps divine.

3. Mani Padme Hum: Sanskrit words. (Bari would later explain to me that they address universal energy.)

4. Om: a sacred utterance that Tibetan and Indian monks chant so that the "m" merges into infinity as a symbol of the absolute, just as the "aleph" sound did for Ibn Arabi.

Bari's charm is a magical prayer of various words from various languages and different times. It tells of an encyclopedic mind and an identity as that of Rumi's—not Muslim, Jewish, Christian, Pagan, or anything else, but all of those things. A magical prayer to God or Energy or the Cosmos, for the sake of Bari, the innocent, pure, and virtuous. Energy is universal, in every place, in the "m" and in Bari, in stars, and in names. He's a creature who sculpts the edges of galaxies, his consciousness is astral, galactic.

In another entry I wrote: His hand placement under his belly—in Oriental wisdom, the universe and the body are an assortment of energies, and the body has energy pathways (hence acupuncture). Along those energy pathways are stations or centers, each is a chakra. The stomach is the center of will. It looks like Bari tries to lift his will with his right hand. In the Quran, on Judgment Day, some hold their book of deeds with their right hand, some with their left. Bari's belly is his book.

Those were samples from my little dictionary. I organized them and planned a trick, a Trojan horse, a war of deception through which I'd lead Bari's heart to its edge, so that his red snail would talk to me: after a round of chess in Last Exit, after a crushing defeat, he would imagine that some external force, demons, ghosts, gods, or whatever, had interfered with his mind, disrupted his concentration, clouded his vision. He would place his right hand under his belly, mutter his charm, do his magical move, expel those forces. That would be the moment I'd drive his heart to the edge—what flood may come.

I was attentive to the opportunity, so it came. I observed him as he lost, his face changing colors. And when he put his right hand at the bottom of his stomach, lifted it, and was about to mutter his charm, I interrupted his ritual and said: "Return the blue light naked to its house." I'd heard this phrase from him, a far greater labyrinth to me than his "Om" prayer, which seemed like child's play in comparison. My sense was that the "blue light" bit touched the depths of his soul, awakened unknown forces.

What I said ran through him like poison. And he lost it.

He swiped the chess pieces off the board, angrily rolled a cigarette, leaned back against a wooden chair, and stared for what felt to me like an eternity. Suddenly he leaned toward me. I felt his breath on my face, his eyes into mine, and he stressed every letter: "Man, I have not spoken with anyone for five years, and here you are talking with me, what are your intentions?"

I mimed him, got my eyes further into him, and stressed every letter: "Listen, man, I am not Moses. I don't ask God to speak his speech to me. But in my life I have arrived at an illicit zone. In front of me are wire fences and a twilight unlike any other in a forbidden land. I am terrified of losing my mind. I can't go back to where I came from, and crossing the fence might mean madness, and you live behind that fence, so what's there?" He spit his loose tobacco and drifted again, then placed his right hand on the table, stood up, and I felt that I might never see him again. "I invite you to my house," he said abruptly, "tonight, you will learn something, I invite you to my house."

The air was fresh, wounding, and cold as we walked down University Way. The asphalt was washed with the rain and the mist of neon lights on metal posts. Everything looked fresh. The asphalt was a black, shiny mirror that tapers into the distance, and I could see my face in the gutters. Bari walked on the surface of this dark mirror as a horse. "I am a load of dynamite," he said, "and when my current life ends, I will explode, boom, boom! I will send the blue light naked to its home! My mind is pure gold, the gold of pure gold. Many others ended up in mental hospitals, but not me, because I am of pure gold, I heal and keep on healing. Tonight, you will learn something, my mind is gold." His repetition of "pure," as in his prayer, caught my attention. "Pure Bari" means a mind of gold free of residue. I was silently and intently listening, didn't say much, spoke only to ask, asked only to know, not to argue about anything, whatever it was.

—What's the mind? I asked.

—The mind? Oh, man, it's horrifying. See . . .

He gestured to the neon light, the asphalt, the skyscrapers, the pier, the closed supermarket, the university library, and said, "That's the mind." I sensed a magical breath course through all these things that we call things. I remembered that American professor in Ramallah who used to stand on his balcony for hours, late at night, under the spell of vacant, yellow-lit streets. He was unaware that he was observing the mind.

I used to think the mind was present in brain tissue, within me, but here it was in the streets and neon lights. In its overflow,

I felt how great the mind was. I looked around me astonished, "This is the mind," I kept repeating. I asked Bari: "Are you inside the mind, then, like Jonah was inside the whale?" "We are in it, and it is in us," he said, "just look at Last Exit, man, what is it, a cafe?" "Yes," I said, "a cafe, wooden tables, kerosene lamps, and wall paintings." "No, no," Bari said, "it was a dream in the owner's mind. He built it, and now we play chess inside the owner's dream, in the hallways of another dream. Imagine! There's a separate, illuminated galaxy that spins around its axis and swims inside each consciousness."

I pointed to the lit skyscrapers in the distance near the wharf, that abstract altitudinous geometry, erect like a taciturn miracle, indifferent, it seeks to increase the distance between itself and neighboring structures, climbs the sky to suggest the power of banks and multinational corporations, a transcendent design of a protestant spirit: "What do you think of those who believe the mind is a riddle no one can see?" I asked. "Don't believe in their keys," he answered.

We reached a back alley with trash and shadows of artificial light. He asked me to wait for him, and disappeared into the alley. I was alone like an idiot, didn't know what to do with myself or his instruction. He came back. "Where did you go?" I asked. He said, "I have a temple here." He has a temple? In a back alley? "I turn myself into a rose bouquet at her entrance," he said. "Who's she?" "The lady," he said.

The closest thing this lady could have been was a woman he was in love with. That's what I thought. But later I realized "the lady" was "the heart." He revealed this in one of his most beautiful designs of madness: "The mind is at the lady's service." "And who's the lady?" "The heart."

Finally, we reached a house, American-style: worn-out wooden doorsteps that led to a glass door. The floor to the reception room was a dirty blue carpet. There was a large wooden table and chairs in front of a large window. To the left, against the wall, an old guitar. To the right, a kitchen door near the stairs to the second floor. Bari went into the kitchen, turned on an electric stove to fry some eggs in a black pan. The oil was bubbling when he spoke again: "My teacher visited me last night and sat in this pan, said he wanted to have dinner with me. I told him to get out of the pan because I didn't have enough eggs for both of us. He refused. I told him that I'd fry him, I swore I would. He refused to leave. Can you believe it? He sat there in the frying pan."

—What did you do?

—I fried him.

He burst out laughing. At that moment I felt he was certified crazy, but when we sat at the table, I felt I was with a mad genius. He said, "Many students knock on my door, their hands like rain, asking me to teach them but they don't understand my words. My experiences are my temple, and my temple is sacred. I let them inside my temple, but they don't comprehend me and end up as stains on my temple's curtains. My teacher could have taught me how to dive before he tossed me into his sea. If he ever comes back and I catch him, I will kill him. Forgiveness is not one of my virtues. Imagine this: yesterday I was fully naked, and Ms. Universe was in my bed naked, and we were about to get it on when my teacher came, shoved me aside, took her, slept with her in front of me. He has no sense of shame, no decency. He took her."

—Who's your teacher?

—A Sufi from Konya.

—Sorry, but I don't get it. Do you mean he literally came from Konya and sat in the frying pan, for example?

—No, no. Each person has two bodies. A mental one and a physical one. My teacher's physical body resides now in Konya, in Turkey. His mental body visits me. His image reaches me from Konya to Seattle. That's how I recollect him. He's in disguise but sends me his spirit. Have you had someone close to you die?

—My father and my little brother. The latter was buried in a cave. Palestine is a land of caves.

—Have you dreamed of your father after his death?

—Sometimes.

—That's his mental body that leaves his grave to visit you.

—Why does he come back?

—Wow! That's a whole other story. But if a face visits you, contemplate its features and detect its intentions.

—The other day you told me that my blue bird visited you at night.

—Yes, your soul did.

—Why was a blue bird my disguise?

—That's an unknown I won't discuss with you, but I contemplated her, your bird, and why she came. Detect the intentions of your visitors, Hussein!

Out of the blue I noticed an emaciated giant coming down the stairs from the second floor. A mass of bones with a yellow face, taut like a drumskin. Suspended eyes that gawked at a horizon, an emptiness, wide wacky eyes, devoid of light, life, or motion, and extinguished. He was very slow coming down. His footsteps were steady toward the reception room, then toward the door. Bari eyed him a bit, then started rolling a cigarette, spitting its loose tobacco: "I tell you, man," Bari said to me, "Dostoevsky's world is for real. Here is a case visited by too many mental bodies." "And how does he see?" I asked. "With the third eye."

My mind drifted to the culture of the dead in Palestine: So many in Palestine die hanged, slaughtered, poisoned, shot, shelled, so many other means. The survivors are visited by the mental bodies of their dead who share their dinners, sit in the frying pan. Ghosts visit me—the ghosts of my father, my brother, my friend. Years ago, a friend of mine took a shower, combed his hair, put cologne on, and went to bed. In the morning he went out to demonstrate against the Israeli occupation, and was killed. I was terrified, less so from his death than from the fact that he was preparing himself for death. These spirits visit me long after their bones had turned to eyeliner dust in a land where the dead dominate the living, the past governs the future. That's the authority of memory in a region whose depth is measured not by centuries but by millennia. Memory is a dangerous thing, a laboratory of ghosts. Didn't Ishtar, a few thousand years ago, in the epic of Gilgamesh, didn't she threaten to "open the gates to the underworld" and let the dead share their meals with the living? We can't live with this kind of deep memory and can't live without memory either, so what's the solution?

—Open your third eye.

—How?

"In Tibet, they open it surgically." He burst out laughing again, perhaps in mockery of my question. He seemed to refer to "The Necklace of Clear Understanding."

The glass door opened, and several teenagers came in. Bari lived in a group housing. Bedrooms were upstairs, to each tenant a room. Bathrooms, living room, kitchen were shared. I didn't know who those teenagers were and why they came? Bari looked like he knew. He didn't speak to them, or they to him. They were six or seven drinking beer and shouting. Each of them had a punk haircut: half the head was shaved, the other half dyed some fiery blue color, or the whole head was shaved except for a flamboyant mohawk, a rooster's crest, orange, yellow, or purple. A surrealist painting. An expanded imagination. Each teenager seeking difference. And yet the irony was that they all looked alike in their search for difference, in their appearance and manners, even in their speech. A while back, when I first met Suzan, she told me: "Welcome to the theory of number one." "And what's that?" I asked. She laughed and said: "I am first, I am second, I am third, and I am tenth, to infinity."

One of the teenagers, a girl with a child's face, was trying to act mature. She looked like Seattle, the city which tries to appear like a big city, like New York. I once asked a New York playwright what he thought of Seattle. He said: "New York is a woman. Seattle is a girl." It occurred to me that no Arab city in Palestine deserves its title as city. In our villages and towns, we have girls, no women, and boys, no men, while people nightmarishly resemble each other. Here each person is a world. That teenager had on a black ballet leotard. Contorting seductively, she lay on the dirty blue carpet, rolling, moaning, sighing. Then, an unforgettable scene whose gesture and strangeness no world cinema could capture: the walking emaciated giant reached the contorting girl, and with remarkable slowness, raised his foot while he gazed into another world, crossed over her, and walked away. Neither thought anything of it.

I recalled a schizophrenic young woman who said this to me about the United States: "Here, you can go to hell, but alone, and you will actually go, and no one will care." Bari and I were observing the proceedings in the common room. He said: "I love this American culture, man. But it is the loneliest in the world. Americans are terrified of loneliness."

I was tense, exhausted, suffocated from too much smoking, too much American coffee which turns my heartbeat into a scrambled TV screen pumping irregular electronic signals. "I'll go out for a stroll in the woods around campus," I said, "maybe I'll come back tomorrow night."

The trails in the woods were organized, elegant, neon lit. There the trees turned into dim shadowy masses sprinkled by ghostly whiteness. Perhaps my upbringing in exposed, arid, rocky highlands with olive terraces, short trees under a burning blue sky, had created within me a dry, open, mountainous emptiness. I never saw the desert as a child, but the memory of the desert space lived in me through poetry: the sea, the desert, beauty, tents, palm trees, oases are foundational in the memory of Arabic poetry, "the sea's blue on the edge of yellow sand," a blue space and a sandy one. Maybe that's why I felt smothered by woods that besiege the skin, close up place around me, conceal a criminal holding a knife, a corpse under packed wet leaves, and I became a secretive guard of myself on constant military alert. The near-endless rain, the tedious greenery that was more a verdant hell than a fertile beauty, my skin that was used to sun and dryness became estranged. When early Arabs introduced the first palm tree to Europe, they called it "the stranger." I was a stranger palm tree.

On my wandering strolls I found a spot in the woods that became my temple: I used to sit on redbrick steps that led to a bolted door. The trees there were more dispersed. And when the moon shone, or when the sky was clear, more spaces between the branches opened up for my eyes, and the branches transformed into black lines on a canvas, an echo of what Gibran wrote: "Trees are a poetry the earth composes on the page of sky. We cut down trees for paper on which we document our emptiness." I used to get lost for hours in that space. Occasionally a music from a piano would reach me through an illuminated window accompanied by a woman's beautiful operatic voice in training. Then a silence would follow. That silence I revered the most.

That night I went to that spot, recalled some of my conversation with the Sufi, and spoke to him: "God is now a silent force. Since the Quran was revealed, nothing else's been revealed."

The Sufi said, "I will write a book on the force of silence."

I said, "But my head is the only thing that doesn't rest. I think and think and think."

He said, "Your intellect is a chimp that jumps over piano keys."

"Only exhaustion from continuous walking silences the mind. Yes, this persistent exhaustion that sits me on these steps," I said, "and what a miserable mind it is that does not listen to what's outside it, doesn't rest, and always engages itself."

"The intellect is a scorpion that can sting itself," the Sufi said. "They've bit your mind, man, bit it as if it were a sheep hung on a tree to sate a wolfpack, or a boxing ball in a training gym."

—Who's "they"?

—They who live in your head, the biting experts.

If only the mind's sea would quiet and learn from God's silence. I felt like a frog. I needed a woman badly, at any cost. Then it occurred to me that Bari himself was no different than the Church of Dianetics or any propagandist of a political party, a nation, class or sect or ethnicity: he wanted to control my mind. He might even have been a secret agent.

Pissed off, I headed back to his house. He was stretched out on his back on the dirty blue carpet downstairs, the back of his head resting in his palms, looking at the ceiling. "Hi, Hussein, you came." "Yes, I came. You're trying to control my mind, man." He sat up, "It is the attribute of a higher mind to dominate a lower one. If your mind is not a lower mind, you should not fear such a thing. And if it is, then it is within my privileges to dominate it. You can also leave."

—No, I will stay. Let's see if you can control it.

I was boiling. He got up to the kitchen.

—Want some tea?

—Why? You're celebrating your conquest of a lower mind prematurely, don't you think?

—Don't tell me what I think. Didn't Walt Whitman say that his best students are those who learn from him how to slay their masters? So, I taught you well. You're standing up to me. That's fine. Have some tea. Maybe I am celebrating my death or the control of your mind. Drink!

I'd never seen worse arrogance. I took the tea cup up to the second floor and he followed me. I wanted to see his room. I was an expert at reading a person's psyche through their furniture and decor. He sped up ahead of me, opened the door, and let me in. The first thing that surprised me was a table with a bright green explosion of a cardboard painting on it, lines and waves of a Van Gogh madness, but it was Bari's own. Out of the green volcano, a black and white square appeared to float on the waves.

I took a closer, more astonished look: it was Bari's face cut out of a camera shot, his eyes gaping at the nutty mass of color that rose like waves around him. To the right of the painting, a metal bed with some kind of mattress. The rest of the room was empty with clean corners. I returned to the painting. Something hit me in the stomach, a meta-human sorrow. I went down to the reception area, resisting the urge to cry, my chest tightening. "Why did you go up to my room?" he asked. "I spent my childhood mostly with my mother," I said. "My father was a migrant worker in Beirut. Sometimes he visited us, other times we visited him. He remained a kind of a stranger to me. My mom never stood in my way. I roamed the mountains as I wished, did what I wanted, and I still feel people's homes are open terrain like the mountains." He laughed, "Man, they didn't extinguish your curiosity, you still have a monkey's instinct."

—And you, you're not a monkey?

—Me? No. You know why? Because I evolve, man. Each night I've got some new thing going on. I barely know who I become.

At a late hour we went to have some coffee at the university hotel. There was no one sitting there. Through a wide glass I watched the soft rain in the street. Bari said that I don't enjoy my coffee, I only gulp it down. He examined a painting on the wall over the bar, a cheap painting I'd seen before. "What's this?" he asked. "Very cheap," I said. "I didn't ask about its price," he said. "It's of an old man drinking coffee," I replied without bothering to take a second look.

"Look at it, Hussein." He got up to it, placed his finger on a spot and began to move his finger: "This edge of the coffee cup has a green line on it, and the cup has the shape of a hat, and this is an old shoe." He spoke as if I were a stupid pupil in the first grade. "Did you notice the old man's pleasure in sipping his coffee?" "No," I said. "What about black, the hat's color?" "No," I said. "That's because you're blind, man. There's no vision free of detail!" "A cheap painting, and I don't need its details," I shot back. He walked back to me upset: "Listen, you have homework tonight. Get in your bathroom, turn the shower full on, and watch the water until morning. Do you hear me? Until morning."

I left upset, without reply. Unaware, I found myself doing what he asked me to do. I sat on the cold edge of the tub, turned on the shower, all the faucets, watched the water until morning. A huge gap between my mind and the water's flow:

my mind is solid, rigid, stationary like the mountains I grew up in, whereas water flows, roars, takes on shapes. I felt my skin turn cold. I started to shiver. I took out a piece of paper and jotted down a poem that flowed out of me. I was ecstatic. I flew to Last Exit with paper in hand. The cafe was closed, so I waited until it opened and Bari showed up as usual. He asked me for two bucks for coffee and I read the poem to him. He snatched the paper. This was an anger I'd not seen in him before. "What's this, man," he said, "I asked you to observe water and you wrote a poem about water. Do you see only to write? To hell with poetry. Watch the water."

He tore the paper and tossed the shreds over my head. I lost my mind. I grabbed him by the collar and screamed: "Don't you dare ever again to touch a paper I'd written on." I was close to punching him. "Man, your I is larger than Seattle," he said as he rolled another cigarette calmly. When I was calm again, he went on: "Observe the water to understand what most people don't understand, something called transformation. Observe the water to understand insanity." The sentence jolted me. I said nothing, gathered the shreds and reread the poem. As he watched me, he was full of love: "Hussein, give me that." He read the poem, pencil in hand. "These reflections are trash. Only one sentence is worthwhile," and he underlined it with his pencil: *Be a waterfall and be a fish*. "But do you understand what you wrote?" "I tried," I said, "but couldn't come up with an answer." He drew a fish with an open mouth on the paper: "This is a fish. Be a fish. Period." And I didn't understand.

At night, I went back to observe water, forgot about poetry. I was spent, sleepless for days. Countless thoughts went through me as I watched water while shivering from spray and splatter. I dozed off at the edge of the tub and dreamt that I was a fish at the bottom of the sea. Above me was a transparent liquid ceiling with a green hue as my mouth opened and closed catching sea crumbs. There were schools of colorful fish swimming in the opposite direction. I swam, swam, swam until I passed by a submerged copper city I'd read about in *A Thousand and One Nights*, just as I'd read about the octopus staring at me from a cavemouth. And there was a stone house that looked like my childhood home as I swam, swam, swam, from one world to another. The next day I discussed the dream with Bari. He spoke first.

—Is a fish only a fish when it swims in the sea but not in a glass or a tub?

—No.

—What if a fish can only swim in a pond but can't else-where, is it still a fish?

—No.

—Why not?

—Because a fish swims in any water.

—That's comprehension. Your golden fish. Its nature is to swim in every theory, each experience, every opinion, any kind of knowledge, any water, but it remains itself: a golden fish. It's the nature of the mind to understand itself, just as it is the nature of a fish to swim.

—And where does the mind swim?

—In itself: it's the waterfall and the fish that swims in that water. Do you get now what you wrote: Be a waterfall and be a fish?

—Yes.

—Why didn't you get it earlier?

—I don't know.

—Because you don't contemplate the universe.

—What's contemplation?

—To contemplate yourself is to comprehend what you always knew without comprehension. Your heart always knew the meaning of "Be a fish and be a waterfall" even before you wrote it, but you didn't understand what you knew.

—Bari, let me ask you about something decisive for me: You know what, I am terrified of madness, of going insane, how do I get out of it?

—Don't rush.

He grabbed his pencil and on the back of a small piece of paper wrote a poem:

Life is a game of chess,
your mind in it is the board,
the pieces, the players, the game, and the rules,
so understand or else
you're an idiot at precisely one o'clock.

CHAPTER TWO

Strange how place appears like a ruse, sometimes, and ruse a labyrinth. I met that Sufi from Konya in the winter of 1998. He was a sea, and I thought he had a bottom, but there was none, only water, no matter how clear, it fell into fathoms only his creator could detect. Perhaps the most accurate description of him is what Suzan said to me in Grand Illusion: "Bari? A creature like King Kong, larger than life." His energy was terrifying: one time he talked from two in the afternoon until six the following morning. I spent sleepless night after night by his side. They were the most intense of my anxious nights. I almost collapsed. I suffered vertigo from so much American coffee, cigarettes, and focus. Then at some invisible moment I couldn't take it any more, decided to go home: "I haven't slept in two centuries," I told him.

He was rolling his Osman tobacco, stopped quizzically, and with a delight that resembled a Dionysian dance, a God crossing valleys and springs under the sun with naked, twirling, inebriated women on his trail, he said: "We're counted among the eternal, man, and you have yet to talk to me about you!"—as if he were reproaching me on the idea of sleep, an ephemerality. I was happy that he included me in his "we," which meant we belonged to a unified superior world in which he asked me to speak with him about myself, from one eternal man to another. My chest puffed with egotism. He looked at me in despair: "I don't like self-congratulatory parties." Praise used to inflate me, and censure deflate me. His comment stung me, and I walked away for a stroll in the woods near campus.

I sat on the edge of a round pond with murky, filthy water on whose surface floated fallen leaves and neon lights. Slowly the ducks swam across this pond of a dormant fountain, its single metal rod. I was exhausted, and occupied myself with observing the ducks until unexpectedly, while fully alert, I experienced a peculiar and stunning vision.

Small stars, illuminated by intrinsic light, revealed their volcanic landscape and scattered tiny craters: six or seven stars at the height of the universe on a mysterious morning that felt like an unborn promise, a transparent verdancy below a glistening blackness like a mirror's. The stars, recently washed with hot water and soap, appeared close, fresh, clean. They released steam. Then my body became that glistening high darkness that contemplates the universe below, before land or sky was formed. I did a double take, shook my head twice in vain: the vision lingered.

Then another vision ambushed me (and this one was destined to accompany me for years): a high sky, like a painting whose faint blue fades here and there into a whiteness. The paint was so old it had cracked. Below it I saw myself as a gray falcon, soaring high, diagonally fast, and able to see the whole land of my memory: its climate, topography, and beginnings. The falcon was watching with a neutrality I hadn't known and couldn't name. He interfered in nothing. He just saw and understood and passed through. Then he spotted me on the edge of the fountain and hovered in the blueness above. I looked up, and our eyes met. He seemed to be observing me in silence before proceeding to fly toward what I have not yet become.

These visions perplexed me. Bari perplexed me more. He who doesn't deeply change me doesn't truly puzzle me. Anyway, that night I went back to Bari's house and spoke with him about . . . about what?

About Some of What the Falcon Saw:

As a boy in the mountains, I loved to take out our mule, Um Iskander, as my father called her, to graze. Everywhere Um Iskander and I went, my uncle's dog followed. I loved to rest in the shade of olive trees with my feet in the cool dirt and stare west, into the distance toward the Mediterranean Sea. Back then, I never got to see the sea up close. Israel dispossessed the coastal plains before I was born, stole the mountain routes to the sea. High noon, deep wild silence, cicadas, shade, olive orchards on soft rounded feminine slopes with flat areolar peaks. Those were the constituents of my memory, their transcendent weather and landscape. In summer, down in the wadi, I saw only the high blue, rocks, short trees that were closer to white and gray than to green groves, and the far, far horizon.

When I saw the sea for the first time in Beirut, I sat far from it, submersed in its roar and damp scent, in a blue fog and a white foamy astonishment. Then on the sea's edge, where spume made landfall, I walked and walked until I could only see the backs of waves rising and falling beyond the distance. You can find the femininity of mountains in the waves, but mountains are fixed, the essence of their consciousness is this fixity: "We've made mountains into pegs," and pegs are triangular, whereas waves are endless forms. The colors, however: the only blue in my mountains was in the sky above, in windows splattered with faint blue paint, in sprinkled flowers, and in some of my clothes that my mother used to wash with some Nile-colored detergent that turned me into a marine creature. I was the memory of landlocked terrain, and the sea was rearranging my memory. I still remember my mother's face in the evening standing over the rocks of the Military Club Pool, my second encounter with the sea. She was wearing a black veil as was the habit of women in our clan back then. The air softly pressed against her face as if against a statue. She, mountain woman, removed her veil and revealed to the sea her primitive, dark face, with its mysterious, deep furrows and tightly sealed mouth. The breeze frolicked with her veil, the sea was closer to black, and its hum rose and fell then rose into a roar.

She showed the sea a different face, so the sea showed her another face: her animal fear of drowning. I would have almost drowned that night had she not pulled me out. I'd not experienced a force of death that powerful nor smelled its scent nor heard its black roar nor sensed a torment such as that. The sea's sunny blue, its spume and vastness, its fog, all seemed to me a veil for primal death instincts. Was Odysseus a sign of the schism within beauty in this world, the rupture that ancient Arabs coined in one word, a "terrific" tossing of terror in the soul that trembles the heart, wobbles it, and also touches absolute beauty?

For years after that, the sea chased me in my dreams, but the mountain child never unified with the sea. He used to wake up drenched in salty sweat as if the sea was seeping out of his clay-pot body. Each time I saw the sea, I felt something similar, a touch of madness. Even when I was four years old and saw the sea from "above," I felt possessed. At the end of the Fifties, American Marines intervened in the first Lebanese Civil War and "evacuated" me and my parents from Beirut aboard a plane for "foreign residents." I looked down through the plane's window and noticed small red and white buildings like Lego pieces interspersed with black, winding streets and little colorful cars running through them. I loved Beirut in that moment, imagined it as a city for children. I wanted to disembark and play in it. But the blue shadow that surrounded it, I had no name for. From the plane, the blue was immobile and vast, and I had no idea that it was the sea. That was my first memory, my absolute first, of anything. Before it I remember nothing.

Possessed by a fascination with a secret city for children no one had told me about and I had not spoken of to anyone, I shared my secret with myself and fell in love with the city. I knew it existed, but where? I looked for it in the mountains. I dragged our mule in search of it, and our dog followed us. I didn't find the city in the shade of olive trees or in the wadis. I didn't spot it when I looked west toward the sea. I used to ride the bus from our village to Ramallah, and sit on the right side to observe the mountain paths that might lead me to my city. On the way back, I'd sit on the left side. Even in April, the cruelest month, when memories mix with desires, I couldn't find my city.

Fifteen whole years passed before I realized I was chasing another marine illusion. I was an undergraduate in Budapest in the school of economics, lived on the bank of the Danube, listened to classical European music, imagined myself in the mountains of my childhood: dark blue. I saw myself at the bottom of a deep valley there, my body a gelatinous mass of a blue embryo trying to be born, restless, pulsing whole as if he were all heart, has a voice, and nothing else. But he remained who he was: a gelatinous mass in the blue mountains. I sensed a blue march in my soul. Shadows like sea shadows.

Those days I heard the music of the Blue Danube. I had stopped dreaming of the city of children and the sea that gave chase to me. In a chase there is movement, energy, vigor, anger, freedom, drama, flare, madness. When the sea quieted, all those feelings drowned like a ball of fire in water. Where did this old, lifeless blue monster go with its context of ash and totalitarian sovereignty? It disappeared in my stomach, I think, and in my muscles, became inertia as I began to turn into a desert, salt white, glistening at noon in mirage mirrors.

Visions of madness intensified in me. I imagined myself in a vacant city, empty of people, a city of red copper I'd read about in *A Thousand and One Nights*: copper sidewalks, shops made of copper, copper trees, and when sometimes at night I strolled in it, the city lights were green, intense green, and wherever I looked, there were mirrors and more mirrors, and not a soul.

A vagabond in green light, I ambled around the suburbs of madness, cohabitated with gypsum statues of naked women around every corner, gypsum that had turned yellow and dirty, statues that stared at me and chased me with their eyes. I did not dream these statues in sleep. They were visions in daylight. Pure imagination, yes, but alive in my depths.

Or I did dream me imprisoned in a sealed, circular glass tower on top of a mountain that overlooks sunny green forests: some hidden hand pulls a trigger, releases a bullet into my head—a slight droning follows, then I fall, and the tower shatters, slowly explodes in cinematic speed, crumbles, as I fall in it and along with it, with my gaze fixed on the sunny green forests. In an earlier vision, I used to see colored lanterns, green, yellow, blue, buried under the dirt paths I walked. I wasn't afraid of madness then. It never occurred to me that I'd go mad, and maybe that was a sign of madness.

My mind had expanded past any limit that could be considered reasonable. Within three years I'd learned a lot of things in various, perhaps disparate fields: philosophy, psychology, political economics, literature, history, mythology, advanced mathematics, architecture, literary criticism, political science, state finance, and music.

In the summer of 1975, I went back to visit my family in Palestine. High noon: ashen dirt that revolts around my footsteps. People with bronze skin under a Mediterranean sun. Bright black or blond hair. Strange features, laughter, teeth. Even their Arabic was strange. In my dreams I spoke Hungarian.

It seemed my comprehension had flipped: my family were the strangers. And those folks, my relatives and friends, seemed to come out of Assyrian times or out of caves that preceded memory. I was stricken with a bout of unrecognition. I didn't, for example, identify a short, chubby, blond, young man who laughed and gesticulated as he sat across from me. I might had seen him in a previous life, but where? Who was he? Half an hour passed before his name came to me: Zeir, a cousin of mine, we grew up together, went to school together all the way through high school. We'd only been apart for three years since. I wasn't sure it was him. "Are you Zeir?" I asked him. He looked at me for a long confused while before he said, "Yes, I am."

Two days after my arrival from Budapest, my father kicked me out of the house. I didn't recognize him as my father, or his house as my house, or as a house. He quarreled, per routine, with my mother over something, and I told him: "Consider me a hotel guest, disinterested in what happens in it." So he kicked me out. Back to Hungary.

I used to long for a country, for a home, a terrain in memory, a referent to aid me in exile and wandering. I longed for something stable, permanent, unchangeable, that can't be lost, forever extant. I was someone who lived in lands built on the back of a whale: they had palm trees, sailors, gold markets, slaves—labyrinthine lands they might have been, but constant, nonetheless. Then the whale suddenly dove toward the depths, and everything seemed to sink, the idea of stability drowned. My world became a tumultuous, shoreless sea, settled by pirates on ships.

I decided to quit the university and travel where I could. A mature Hungarian woman who worked at the university president's office asked me: "Have you read *War and Peace*?" "No. Why?" I said. She said: "You remind me of character in it, a guy called Pierre." "I don't know him," I said then grabbed a pencil and sketched innumerable concentric circles, pointed to a spot in the middle, and said, "I'm roughly here." I'll never forget her reply: "As long as you kind of know where you are, there's no problem. One day, maybe twenty-five years from now, send me a letter to tell me what's happened with you. I'd like to know."

I read *War and Peace* and liked this Pierre guy. He resembled an apartment during a war: stairs break, windows burn, doors come unhinged, but inside Pierre there's always an unharmed wing, a room fit for living.

Eight full years later, I arrived in Seattle, in December 1985, to study comparative literature at the University of Washington, the third university I had enrolled in. I arrived a few days before Christmas, with nothing to do. I thought of writing that Hungarian woman a letter, but I'd lost her address.

I stayed at the YMCA near the pier. To entertain myself, I set to observing people. One time a man with mental illness walked through the glass doors into the lobby talking to himself, signaling, laughing, singing his heart out. Abruptly he turned toward me, bowed twice and spoke: "I am sorry, sir, I am really, really sorry." I'd not seen him before. I had no idea what his apology was about, or why he thought I was a Catholic priest for the confession of his sins. "A space case," said an American electrician in a pair of jeans and a beer in hand. I liked the expression, "space case," and added to it: "crushed by a mysterious guilt."

A feeling that also crushes me. When my father died of a stroke in the late Seventies of the last century, they laid him in a casket of old wood, and shrouded him in white. Friends and family stood single file to extend their farewell. Each with a sad look or a kiss on his forehead. My sister, the one whose hair we washed in sea water at the Military Club Pool in Beirut, threw herself on him and started to wail. They pulled her off his corpse by force so that she might not fully collapse. My turn came. His face was pale yellow and ghostly white, inhabited by an ancient rage and bizarre dark green spots that looked rotten. It gave me pause. I stood like a stone statue, immovable, no kiss.

My mother pushed me in the back. I didn't move. As long as I lived, I said to myself, I don't want the taste of death on my lips, and then walked away. My father died and I didn't even kiss him in his casket. A blue guilt like that of a blues song, painful and writhing, oozed into me. A song recorded on my lips. Have you ever heard of lips that feel guilty? My lips do. If I draw them, they'd look like a peculiar mix of green, yellow, and dry, cracked white. After that I was afraid to talk. A French woman painter told me once: "Either way, you lose, if you speak or don't."

Months after my father's death, I began to run away from myself, my speech, found myself in another city, another continent, another time: Iowa, USA, 1979, married to Mary (not her real name), a woman with schizophrenia.

I met her in a hotel lobby. She was paying her rent out of her Social Security check, unable to adapt to a work environment, totally lonely, dominated by her past in New York. Whenever a schizophrenic hallucination attacked her, her eyes would widen behind her round glasses, and she'd look like she'd seen something invisible that would turn her gaze left and right before she'd dart into another room, shut the door behind her. She told me that during such moments she often heard a criminal with a New York accent threaten her from inside the heater in the room. Other times she'd hear running water in the bathroom warn her of an upcoming event.

She had a recurrent dream. She would flee barefoot in intense rain across an abandoned bridge over some river, lightning flashing all around her, then thunder would speak in a New York accent: "Return to Jesus, your Savior." My analysis was that her disintegrated life was the result of her loss of faith in a country that produces schizophrenics as much as it produces sandwiches.

At the hospital she frequented, I walked the illumined, clean hallways, sat in waiting rooms with color TVs and artificial flowers, saw humans, if one can call them that, whose condition had declined into a mix of ghosts and plants: they called them "vegetables."

With space cases, it seems that God or Destiny or some other force has stuffed a patient in a spaceship and tossed them into deep space, or that the patients were residents of deep space who were sent to Earth by other creatures in their domain. Yet these "vegetables" live in an underworld here on Earth, in one of Dante's circles of Hell for those who were below animals and above inanimate objects, a combination of plants and ghosts, an imagination I'd thought existed only in the mind of filmmakers. (And later, I did see a stunning movie about these "vegetables" called *Awakenings*).

Mary recounted her story. As a girl, she ran away from her parents' home, homeless until she ended up as a volunteer in a remote church in the countryside. She'd arrange the colorful flowers, which the faithful had donated, into bouquets then distribute them to pedestrians on street corners. After seven years of "good deeds," her piety was recognized with a transfer to the central church in New York, the city of great wandering. Mary, the flower nun, after years of living on the Cross of Roses, found herself not in a church but in an operation that ran prostitution and drugs connected to a web of churches. She tried to escape but they injected her with sedatives, held her captive for years in some mansion with watch dogs, swimming pools, and gardens, and when she finally broke down into schizophrenia, they let her go, released her as a ruin to psychiatric specialists, two in particular: her doctor and her mother.

I proposed to marry her, either out of despair or because I was playing the role of a Jesus who offered roses down from his cross to his nuns. Or because I needed to be with a woman at night, no matter the cost. I proposed. And when I thought of rescinding my proposal, she stitched her eyebrows together on the edge of failing to concentrate an idea in her consciousness, and her lips took the form of a beak made of white flesh.

Guilt and pity crushed me. I told her I was kidding. Maybe I sensed that I myself was heading to a schizophrenic existence, with God's help, of course. After marriage, her condition improved a little. My submerged years in "psychology" prepared me to deal with her, since I was also a space case.

Her doctor and her mother invited me to a fancy dinner one night. "How do you treat her?" they asked me. They wanted to understand how it was that with me she took up cooking, running, looking for jobs, restoring what Freud called ego? Where did they fail? "I treat her like a human being," I said. They didn't get what I was saying. "Do you mean that you are a human being or that she is a human being?" they inquired—or that together, hypothetically, as a unit, she and I added up to a human.

Mary used to talk in her sleep, mumble about some helicopter. Several hints led me to understand that she wished I was rich enough to own one. I was, as I am, a broke intellectual. So I bought her a dark blue lamp for her side of the bed. Under that dark light I used to watch her sleep, hear her mumble and dream that she was another woman, Mindy, who would change her voice, dream different dreams, sleep with other men, and cry in her sleep, as I smoked and stared into the blue light. I made sense of much of her hallucinations except for that helicopter bit. Where does the aircraft come from to land in a dream and why? Who's this Mindy? Then Mary invited me to a party at her mother's house.

A middle-class home with a spacious yard, a mowed lawn, and an old wooden fence. I walked around the area and was startled when a helicopter landed in the adjacent lot. The force of sound and air pushed me away close to the fence. Out of the helicopter, a handsome man in a black suit and a beautiful free and gentle blonde woman stepped off. Mary came out of the house running to the copter, embraced the blonde. Strange rituals followed. The blonde raised Mary's foot and kissed the sole of Mary's shoe, then introduced herself to me: "I'm Mindy, Mary's sister." I couldn't believe my eyes. Mary dreams she's her sister. Their mother introduced me to Mindy before I could speak: "This is Hussein, Mary's husband and, of course, he's not a bum." Had I been one, she'd have hidden me in a closet away from the millionaire's eyes.

Mary had a parrot's mind. I had noticed that Mary started her replies to any of my questions with "Good. Mom said," or "Good. Mom asked." I'd ask her: "What do you think of the yellow flowers?" and she'd reply "Good. Mom asked." I'd ask Mary: "What do you think of frozen ice?" and she'd reply: "Good. Mom said." A parrot's mind. In this, she was like her father who repeated one formula as solution to any problem.

If, for example, Mary needed his company for an hour, just one hour, he'd say: "Mary, my love, you feel lonely, and that's your personal problem." And when Mary, hysterical, heard a criminal speak to her in a New York accent through the heater, he'd say: "Mary, my love, you're hearing a criminal from New York and that's your personal problem."

And like her father, Mary was so individual. One time she lost her marbles because I forgot "my coffee" mug on the table in the kitchen. "I am not your servant," she screamed, trembling. In a world drowning in singularity, it is difficult to offer this reply: "Fine, I will clean the table," as this indicates a concession of my individuality in favor of hers. Difficult also to say "Fine, let's clean it together," as this is public abuse of private property. And equally difficult to tell her, "You clean it," as this would be an assault on her individual integrity. So, we agreed that we each clean our half of the table. The table, too, was split in two, its personality a schism.

Those days I took a trip to Chicago. My hotel-room door had three metal bars on the inside, and an unusual bolt, as if sleeping in it risked a death that could only be thwarted by memorizing the number to the police station, written on a small piece of paper and placed on top of the color TV.

Back home, Mary turned to me in terror: "On the same night you left for Chicago, a criminal came to my apartment, tried to break down the door, almost managed it were it not for the inside bolt, and I called the police." A shudder ran through me: if anything had happened, I'd be accused of killing her and fleeing to Chicago. I'd have no chance to escape a life sentence in prison.

I sat at the edge of the bed and thought: perhaps she "imagined" the event. Schizophrenics often envision circumstances of self-persecution. Anyhow, I grew so anxious after those days that I began to suffer bouts of uncontrollable tremor. I had to measure each word, each expression, weigh each dream and movement, consider their effect on her psyche. Her mom and doctor were convinced that I'd married her because I had "no identity," that I didn't know who I was. Maybe they were right, but what "identity" did they give Mary? Her mom turned her into a parrot, her doctor into a "client" who enabled him to have a sexual relationship with her mother.

Then Mary and I got a divorce.

A few years later I was back in Palestine, living in a modern white-stone apartment behind Ramallah's central prison. My fears of madness established their residence in me. I wrote a few lines to my ghost, the other Hussein:

In blue skies you soar, a tin bird
with nothing against or for.
A silk thread, nothing more, binds you to earth,
a wild hare snips it, and you lose your place.

I felt that I'd lost the last thread that tethered me to "reality." I'd shave my beard at night and say to myself in the mirror, "Stay the course."

The Israeli military governor of Ramallah and the West Bank at the time was a man called Menachem Melson. One night in my living room, in front of my scrambled TV and its electronic drizzle in black and white, I read a report on his personality. It frightened me. I spoke to him in my mind and said: "You, too, Menachem Melson, stay the course."

He seemed equally concerned with losing his hold on "reality." His obsession with events, intelligence reports, orders, and all that was necessary to manage and rule the West Bank served only the purpose of proving to himself that he remained connected to "reality." But that reality was like water through his fingers. The more reality slipped and slid, the more his fears grew and his obsession with control (of people and things) intensified. All because he wanted to remain in touch with "reality."

The River Jordan is a silk thread that splits the place in two banks: east and west. Menachem Melson ruled only the west one. The east bank seemed to constantly slip through his fingers. His obsessive desire to dominate it echoed the well-known Zionist song: "Jordan has two banks: the first is ours and the second, too." If a wild hare were to snip the Jordan river, and the Jordan river were to disappear, its two banks vanish, Menachem Melson wouldn't be able to tell his east from his west. History is cunning. To split the personality of a place into two banks is a space case where each personality breaks independently from the other, and yet a connecting passage is needed. Some ploy, this: so it can be said that the two personalities, despite their independence, coexist in the selfsame person, as one body, one patient, one place.

This trickery manifests in a small metal and wooden bridge over the river, a passage and a deception, from west to east, for those whom history has forced through the bottleneck of occupation, and from east to west, for those whom history will force through the bottleneck of occupation. No other way to enter or exit the place but out of one personality and into another, schizophrenically. The "bridge" is an instance of personality exchange: from Mary to Mindy, for example, as the first personality of the schizophrenic is usurped by its other. This is the densest expression of non-place, of Palestine, and of Ramallah, the city Menachem Melson and I lived in.

In that Ramallah, I was penniless and homeless. I knew hunger. To keep myself afloat, I'd drink one or two raw eggs. The most miserable smell is that of raw eggs inside an empty stomach, the stomach of a nicotine-and-anxiety addict. A friend from the college days at Birzeit University invited me to live with a group of students in that modern white-stone apartment behind the central prison—a group that fed me and sheltered me with legendary generosity. A light green couch became my bed in the living room. The living room was my "bridge."

One night I fell asleep and left the TV on, then woke up in terror of some concealed thing in my soul. I looked around. On a wooden chair by the TV was a person who looked like me, an exact copy. He seemed to have been there for a long time, observing me in my sleep. I sensed his presence, his energy in the air around me, as a boy might sense the presence of his deceased father seated in a chair, then sense him in the mirror shaving his beard—(those memories that gather and deepen into energy and conjuring until the boy sees his father in the chair over there as if there's no such thing as death). I was inside another apartment within the white-stone apartment or I was in the presence of another personality of the apartment that had overtaken an earlier one. "Stay the course," I said to myself, "you're trying to imitate the Jordan river and split in two."

In that living room, I wrote the last chapter of my novel, "The Third Bank of the River Jordan." The author was another Hussein who mimicked Menachem Melson who, at night in the mountains, heard the movement of a wild rabbit that snipped the last thread that tethered him to "reality." That night, along with the friend who invited me to live in the apartment, I wrote a few lines of bad poetry we thought were beautiful at the time and offered them as a gift to a Karate instructor we knew:

> I'm about to go into this vacant apartment.
> Give me a call: my other self
> will be waiting by the phone.
> Though if I leave, I'll do so with the resolve
> of the Kharijites, or with Muawiya's deception.

I was on the edge of complete fracture. During my last days in that living room with its black and white tiles, I dreamt I was in a tavern, an American-style wood cabin I'd previously seen in *Once Upon a Time in the West*. It was teetering on the edge of a cliff I didn't recognize. Heavy, the ceiling buckled, and the gutters gave strange sounds as they slid through the ceiling, and in the middle, a yellow light bulb at the end of a black wire swung wildly, alternating the apparition of the damp light it emitted, altering the tavern whose furniture began to glide back and forth in all this wetness. Whenever I tried to latch onto something, it fell, and I found myself on my belly out on the porch, trying to clutch at a smooth wooden floor as if I were clutching at light on wood. And when I managed it, just a little, two boards between my hands and under my face broke, a hole opened up in which I saw bright black waves rise toward me then fall and rise again, and I felt the terror of drowning to death, realized that the tavern was at sea, and I was coming apart.

Oh God how I longed for balance . . .

I remember watching a Chinese-acrobat show on TV: a young woman on her back raised her legs on which other girls built a pyramid with their bodies to reach the high ceiling. Its beauty and balance intrigued me. "It shouldn't surprise you, Hussein," a friend said. "This is Chinese culture. It's been searching for its balance for five thousand years. This is a pyramid born out of history," he explained.

So, Bari, who am I now, other than a madman running through a moonlit mountain in an imbalanced history? Where do I get my hands on a balanced history, Bari? Oh God, not even words are . . .

Bari had been listening to me the whole time. An apprehensive black flash in his eyes. His eyes were two lines of an unknown he hesitated to divulge. I stopped talking. To my surprise, he had no immediate comment. Silently he rolled his cigarette, then said only this: "Your consciousness is social, man. I can stand up to any evil except the social evil." He spit the loose tobacco and went back into contemplative silence.

Behind him was a window with two panes widely open on a transparent, mysterious blue space. Bari appeared sculpted into the frame. I leaned against the window, pondered a robust rose tree by a wooden fence and wondered: "What am I looking for here in this continent?"

A movie recurred to me, about an ancient Chinese monastery. A monk plants a rose tree for a boy to teach him Kung Fu, tells him to jump over it daily. As it grew, the boy's strength grew. He leapt over it like a cat.

Another movie came to mind. This one about the Shaolin temple also in ancient times. Worn out fragments in my memory of a Buddhist monk who'd been teaching a boy, since his tender years and soft nails, the art of Kung Fu. The boy matured into a young man, and the monk handed him a chain with half a golden medallion, and said: "I have nothing more to teach you. Only one person can teach you more than I have. Go to him." He gave the young man the address of this monk, on the other side of China. "How will I know him?" asked the young man. "In his possession is the other half of this medallion," replied the monk.

In the promised city, the young man discovers that the address his teacher gave him does not exist. He wanders the city totally perplexed, encounters a gang that traps him in an open court and nearly kills him. His head begins to spin, he's about to fall, about to die, he stares into his chest and sees, as if in a dream, his teacher from Shaolin calling to him: "You possess the other half. Only you can teach you more than I have taught you."

For years I dreamed of dropping everything in my life for a monastery in China. To learn Kung Fu and never leave the place. But people like me can't give their whole life down to the smallest atom in their heart to anything in the world. People like me are destined to dispersal, to scattering. As with dew on grass, I don't gather into a stream or a river toward an irreversible, definitive direction. I am one of those who live for things only half-heartedly, at best. All my evils come from this half heart, if there's a heart left at all. This condition delivered me to a spiritual desert.

And I remembered, remembered, remembered, all my life was a series of memories, one idea into another into another . . . of my imprecise memories. Usually I alter them, edit them, restore and renovate, invent, etc. I leaned my head against that window with two wide open panes to wash my head in the blue space and remembered nothing.

Bari said nothing. I felt insulted. Angry, I spoke: "Bari, you've said nothing to my words."

—Each person has their dance with life, man, and I can't dance your dance with it.

—My destiny is singular like this rose tree here, and it grows alone and that's lovely and all, but what do you think of my dance, Bari?

He rolled another cigarette capped by another spit then emphasized every letter he spoke: "Distinguish between the mind and its contents, Hussein."

It was the first time I'd heard a distinction such as that. I understood nothing, went back to the table, sat down facing him, stared into him like an imbecile, and long moments of sealed silence passed before I said: "And what's the difference between the mind and its contents?"

A white plate with leftover scrambled eggs, cigarette butts, and French bread lay before him. He grabbed the edge of the plate in disgust, tossed everything on it onto the filthy blue carpet by my feet, then skidded the plate toward me across the table, and pointed to it: "That's the mind," then he pointed to the eggs, cigarettes, bread on the carpet and said: "And that is its content."

—Truth is always palpable, concrete, so be concrete now: What is my mind's content?

—Your mind is a monkey stung by the scorpion of its past and now jumping and screaming, Wah! Wah! That's your mind's content: a monkey screaming.

I imagined myself as a short monkey, holding his right foot and hopping away from the scorpion, screaming in a vast jungle: Wah! Wah! and laughed. "That's about right," I said.

—It's not about right, Hussein, it is right. Your mind is a scorpion-stung monkey. You're like that poor Indian man who came to a temple looking to enlighten his being and began to narrate his past to the monk, his memories and suffering, his need for enlightenment, and he talked and talked. As the monk listened, he poured tea into a cup, kept pouring until the cup overflowed, the tea spilled onto the wooden table, then onto the ground, the monk kept pouring, and the man kept talking until he reached a boredom that made him notice, so he said: "The cup is full. Why do you keep pouring tea?" The monk said: "Your mind is like this cup. Full. Empty it and I will serve you some new tea."

—Do you mean I'm boring?

—Yes, you are. I don't mean to offend you, since knowledge is impersonal, but you are boring. Do you know why? Because your cup is full of your old tea. Empty it.

He got up upset, went to a bookshelf that had a pile of torn and dirty computer print paper he used to collect from the streets. He rummaged through it, found a book buried in it. I found out later it was a book on feminine wisdom in some Indigenous American culture: "Medicine Woman," a synonym in some anthropologic vernacular for witch or sorcerer. He opened the book. I wasn't sure if he was reading from it or simply making it up as he went along. He was staring at the page, yet appeared as if he were staring at an invisible chess board when he reached out and grabbed a fistful of air, raised it slowly toward me and said: "Here's one of your opinions." He turned to the chess board, tossed an imaginary chess piece onto the carpet and, in utter joy combined with a depth in his voice and a humility before a mysterious force, added: "Wow, man, wow! And this here is one of your theories," then tossed a second imaginary chess piece. "And this is one of your memories." A third chess piece. "One of your dreams." A fourth chess piece. "One of your pains." A fifth chess piece. He kept tossing pieces until the chess board was empty. Then he said: "This is called emptying the mind of its content."

I held back from irritating him further. I didn't say, for example, that I still didn't get it. I opted for silence. What he said reached me, but I didn't comprehend it. According to Heraclitus, too much information does not necessarily lead to knowledge. Bari picked up on this, tossed the book away, and spoke in a rage.

—Listen, man. Life is a river. To each his cup to scoop from it. Your cup is small.

Calmly and sarcastically I replied to push his fury to the limit: "And what's my cup?"

He ran into the kitchen, brought back an empty cup, put it in front of my eyes, and shook it: "What's this?" he said.

—A cup.

—Would you call it a cup if you can only pour tea in it but not coffee or juice, for example?

—No.

—And if you can only pour coffee in it, but not water, is it a cup?

—No.

—Why?

—Because a cup naturally contains an empty space, and a space naturally receives whatever I want to pour in it.

—That's the mind. Your golden cup. It's natural for a mind to be empty, and natural for an emptiness to receive any opinion, theory, belief, feeling, memory, or knowledge. Distinguish between the mind and its content just as you distinguish between the cup and the tea in it.

With each of his words, my heart was passing through several worlds. His manner of comprehending things stunned me. He was the first being, or insane person, who didn't discuss with me any of the details of my life I had divulged to him. He signaled to me that I should toss all of my memories in the trash. A human is made of their experience, and my memory was of my experiences. Yet he had previously said this to me: "My experiences are my temple, and my temple is sacred." So, provocatively, I replied: "You contradict yourself. Or do you think I'm stupid?"

He screamed in my face: "I contradict myself? Yes, I contradict myself, so what? My mind is of pure gold, pure gold, man, so do I contradict myself? Yes, I do, so what? My mind is a golden serenity, and I've turned blue in the face trying to explain you to you! This is what I have done for you. What have you done for yourself? Will you waste your life in cafes?"

A deep pain hit my stomach, a deep pain because he spoke a truth I didn't want to see: I used to spend most of my time in cafes, in a trivial river called daily life, and daily life was nothing but an impoverished literary imagination. *Way of the*

Peaceful Warrior taught me that I'm an addict, meaning that I live a life under the spell of habits I have no control over.

—What do I do?

—To do something is to change something. A few years ago, I was at a temple in Haiti. I have prepared you well for it. I know a monk there. His knowledge surpasses mine. A terrific monk, I'm telling you. I'll send you there. He will tell you that I have prepared you well. Go there.

Scattering began to overwhelm me, scattering and fatigue. Another pain struck me out of this Haiti advice, a pain borne of my love for Bari. I excused myself, headed home. He looked at me sadly, shook his head, didn't object.

It was a bit chilly outside, and refreshing. I went to my studio apartment, took a long hot shower as if I were expelling ice from my bones, and yet the external temperature did not come inside. I threw myself into the polyester sleeping bag, tried to doze off. A soft knocking on the glass wall snapped my eyes open. Bari was outside. Reproachful, he spoke: "Man, you sleep forever. Come, let me show you something weird."

His visit and tone surprised me. Something had just happened with him. I got up, followed him. He pointed in some direction toward the back alleys. I followed. He walked and repeated: "Hussein, trust no one, not even me, not even me, trust no one, not even me."

He was shook up, sobbing, wiping his tears with his sleeves, he was agitated, and I followed clueless as to what had happened. Morning broke. We reached a forest with a wide, clear pond. I could see to the bottom. "Look here, here at the bottom," he said. I saw. "See the bottom," he said. I looked again. Confused I looked into his eyes. He dried his tears.

—Hussein, do you see the bottom?

—Yes.

—Is it totally clear?

—Yes.

—Is there any barrier between the surface and the bottom?

—No.

—Nothing?

—No.

Befuddled I stared at him. He pressed his face to mine and emphasized every utterance: "You need this clarity. To see the depth as you see the water at the bottom of this pond. Lesson over."

I understood the lesson. It was a good one. But what was the secret of his tears? One time he cried, and I asked why. "Over this fallen humanity," he replied. But that was an answer to an earlier crying. I had no explanation for his current one. He left me at the edge of the pond. I watched him from afar as I watched the pond. Then he stopped, looked my way, saw me still crucified in place, and called out: "Man, in each mind thoughts swim away and only bits remain. Between one thought and another there's a lot to be discovered." He shook his finger as if to say he really meant it.

Those last words turned my stacked soul, its solid mass, into a sieve. Pores opened between one thought and another. My mind grew into scattered islands in a sunny vast ocean: endless knowledge between one island and another. I felt that all I knew was nothing. Isn't that a form of emptying the mind of its contents? Some words filled the mind with their contents. Other words emptied it. The latter type are more beautiful. The mind was the potentialities of the mind and not its contents. Or the mind was as Gibran said: "Man is not judged by his achievement but by what he yearns for." And the mind was a yearning. The mind was a longing for a future. But why did it long for anything? What did a mind want from its longing?

I submerged myself in the polyester sleeping bag. "To see the bottom, without a barrier that disrupts the distance between the surface and the bottom, this is the clarity you need, you need this clarity . . . below . . . " I dozed off for God knows how long.

Two nights passed before I went back to see him at his house. He was with two guests: a tall, thin blond American man with pale skin and a rectangular mustache, seemed kind and ordinary, and another with a dark complexion, well shaven and handsomely dressed, with a round face and red eyes. I thought the latter was a drug addict, and when he spoke, he said: "I don't like to be alone at night in my house. When I'm alone, I see a flock of beautiful naked women slowly pass in front of me, just like that, they pass (he drew a half circle with his hand) in slow motion, and they look at me in silence. I'm not talking about hallucination here, Bari, I swear to you, man, not imagination, but for real, I see them pass, like that . . . "

Bari replied: "I know, man, I know."

Astonished, I asked him: "You know what?"

Bari pointed to the dirty, worn-out, blue carpeted staircase that led to the top floor: "Sometimes down that staircase ugly naked women come, among the ugliest in God's imagination, and I call them the beautiful ones. A courtesy, that's all. God's glory is in his creatures," and he burst out laughing.

"And what do you do with them?" I asked.

"You should ask what they do with me." And he drowned in laughing tears, rolled his cigarette, leaned his face to mine: "I have a golden sense of laughter, man. The gods are serious, and Bari is funny." In that moment I was in the company of a crazy person waking up from his madness by laughing at ghosts or with them. Madness was his country. I felt that to exit the madness, I had to learn this golden laughter. Before Bari, I don't think I knew anyone who laughed. And still I was frightened. My hair stood on end. The blond guy's face also contorted in a fear worse than mine. His skin turned yellow. He said he was going to get a bottle of wine and asked me to join him.

Terrified in the wide empty neon-lit street, he said, "I will hold your hand," and he placed his right hand inside my arm and stuck to me. His name was Joe. I tried to calm him down. I was discombobulated myself. Total insanity was waking up inside me. There I was with the mad and the insane. How was it going to end?

In art, you must touch madness without waking it. And I was touching madness and waking it in life. That's more dangerous. I couldn't return to where I came from, and my hope in exiting that state depended on Bari, period. I needed to learn the art of oscillation between wakefulness and madness. I imagined my lonesome self in my apartment interrupted by a flock of naked women: "What will I do?" I asked myself. "I will flip, go mad, there's no doubt. Even if I think about it and see nothing, I will lose my mind. If only one woman appeared, I'll go insane."

Way of the Peaceful Warrior taught me a useful technique: if crazy thoughts occur to me, "let them pass," don't think of them, instantly forget them. And I would forget them, without analysis and without realizing that I was not thinking of them. I'd let them go as they came. Otherwise "using the mind" in this type of zone is nothing but a new energy that propels madness to its realm.

Still, if I were to see naked women coming down the stairs in another realm, what then? To ask Bari would risk his ire. He'd scream if I asked, "Bari, this world you live in is crazy, how do you get out of it or stay aware?" He'd reply: "Man, you can't insinuate something better than that?" . . . meaning, I shouldn't suggest to him that he's crazy, shouldn't mess with his dormant forces, plant in his head some subconscious, negative thoughts about himself. Or else he might say: "You're one of them who feed on my energy." I had to think of a different formulation to the question. By the time Joe and I returned to Bari's place with a bottle of wine, I had arrived at a reasonable, slant approach, a wily one. After the two guys left, I asked him: "How do you cross a danger zone?"

He rolled another cigarette, spit the tobacco, lit it, and spoke after a silence: "By knowing that I, too, am danger."

An idea flashed in my head that madness was a kind of weakness. To exit it, one must have faith that one was not a prey, but rather a tiger and a tiger hunter, dangerous.

I remembered a night in Ramallah. I woke up on that couch in the living room of the apartment behind the central prison. I was alone. A yellow light outside. Silence. Droning silence. I heard a ghost in the kitchen washing the dishes. A raven female ghost of an evil type. The kitchen door was slightly ajar. I couldn't see. A shiver ran through my skin, an electric fear of what was behind me. I covered my head with the blanket, to no avail. I couldn't convince myself that I was hallucinating. My thoughts of the ghost intensified its presence. I noticed the white karate uniform and the black belt hanging on the wall. I jumped to it, put it on, tightened the belt as I trembled, went to the kitchen screaming: "Not even a ghost will wash my dishes. I won't have it." In the kitchen, silence. I turned on the light, nothing. A humming refrigerator. A dripping faucet. Bread, sink, plates. Nothing out of the ordinary. I drank some tea, went back to bed in my karate uniform.

It was not strange that my will changed from a retreating, scared will to that of an angry warrior who believed in his dangerous capacity. What's strange was that the transformation occurred after I had changed my clothes. In my heart, a karate uniform was linked to strength, to halls of fortified concrete walls in which water collected despite the icy weather outside, and wind entered through high open vents. As I stood in free-combat mode to attack my enemy, sweat poured out of me. That memory itself sleeps in me in a karate uniform, just as knowledge of good and evil used to sleep in a divine apple that Adam and Eve ate from. The uniform's white color or its feel on my skin permitted the flow of force into me, a force that returned a lost memory to me, a memory that I, too, was dangerous. My identity spreads even in my clothes, my warrior identity, that is, not my latent victimhood. Hasan Helwani, my karate instructor, once told me that the strength of my strike depended on my belief in it.

What happened in that Ramallah living room was now clear to me. In those days, I had no money, the clothes I wore weren't mine, and my heart knew before I knew that others' clothes were like a leech that sapped me of strength, weakened me, turned me into a parasite. My strength was in my skin, nowhere else, nothing is more spacious.

And I recalled how Israeli intelligence officers, when they interrogated Palestinian prisoners, would offer them a cigarette. Accepting the cigarette, in the logic of magic, establishes a channel through which the prisoner's identity flows into the interrogator. The prisoner becomes weak. His idea of a sovereign self, independent of the officer, begins to crumble. All that with a cigarette. I also remembered how UNRWA distributes rations to the Palestinian refugees in sacks on which "Aid from the United States" is printed: a sorcery that enfeebles, strips a person of dignity, places them at the mercy of donation from the empire. Since the Stone Age, magic's been the logic of the world.

All orders of magic across history declare as much: the depth of each identity dives in enigmatic rituals: death has rituals, weakness has rituals, holiness too, and politics, birth, maturity, marriage, and writing, each have rituals. Rituals are a suggestive force, like a night fire that hypnotizes whoever stares at it.

In the *Epic of Gilgamesh*, Enkidu—who was nursed by lactating animals in the wild, and whose hair was as long as the goddess of wheat—was a primitive beast, and lost his strength when he slept with a sacred prostitute by a spring in the prairie. He understood knowledge. And knowledge is a weakness, even if "through knowledge you become like a God, Enkidu."

In Uruk, Enkidu had a dream that he died. The council of the gods concluded that he was confirming his manner of death. To see weakness is likely a weakness: he saw others determine his fate, and believed that those others were stronger than he was and more awesome. There he was at the entrance to the Underworld, where he'd feed on dust and clay, when the Anzu bird, a higher being, bewitched him into a lower bird, because Enkidu had become weaker and his bread had turned to clay and dust.

The same went for the moon goddess, Inanna. As she entered through the gates to the Underworld, one by one, each gate stripped her of some of her splendor: her lunar crown, her lazuli staff, her necklaces, her dress, and whenever she asked "Why?" the ghosts told her: "Don't ask, Inanna. These are the rituals of the Underworld." By the depths of deadness she was totally naked, her previous identity erased.

These are the rituals of weakness: strength seeps outside. And my meandering in low places was stripping me of one feature after another with each step I took. That's a sign of the frightened, of one whose will has collapsed, retreated as a red snail into a dubious shell. I used to imagine myself as a wolf sometimes. But instead of attacking the fire of shepherds to usurp what I could, I saw myself standing in the sunset, facing a distant twilight, howling in sorrow on top of a hill. Sorrow is a weakness even if it turns you into a demigod, Enkidu. And pity for yourself or anything is a weakness, even if you are a Christ. And there he was, that Sufi from Konya, pledging another road for me: I should know that I am also dangerous, a danger, another knowledge with antagonistic rituals and contradictory dance.

The stage director, Yakub Ismail, once told me of a crazy boy in Ramallah who loved the prairies. "Why don't you like being with people or being at home?" the boy was asked. He said, "They don't want me to become a god like they are." And there he was, that Sufi from Konya, planting in me a different will: "You can will yourself to become a god like them, your will is most important, and you will become it, just wait a bit, my son, and you will, I swear to you, by the One who has released the two waters that never merge, you will be free one day, through your own will, nothing else. That will be your spoils. It's the kismet the Gods provide for warriors."

—Bari, will you teach me the rituals of being dangerous?

—Be an Indigenous warrior.

—How?

—What's your favorite animal?

—Tiger.

—Fine. Your blue bird came to me one night, do you remember? I don't want it. Send me your tiger.

I felt clueless. So I improvised a pretension: "When?"

—Tomorrow night, exactly at ten. Send him, do you hear?

All his talk was weird. For hours I thought how to send him my tiger at precisely 10 p.m. At last, on the following night, I went to his house. He was waiting, ready, got up from his chair, and spoke as if he were preparing for a military expedition to invade the Great Wall of China.

—Hello. You've come?

—Yes.

Heavily he lifted his right leg, and slowly, forcefully, hit the ground with it as if it were of iron or rock. The floorboards creaked near breaking. Bari began purring like a tiger. I got it. I was to imitate him, walk his way, purr as he did. I saw myself as a Bengal tiger, strolling through a forest. The birds were startled. A thousand monkeys screeched as they climbed up the branches. Gazelles froze distracted and hearkened in fear of my rustling footsteps. I stopped at an overlook by a water spring. A group of kin tigers had gathered below. I went down the hill to meet my folks.

Bari and I sat down for tea: "The first time you invited me to your house," I said, "you told me you had a temple in a dark back alley where a woman lives, and you become a bouquet of roses for her. Who or what is she?"

—Where your heart resides, it creates a temple for you. There's a woman in my temple. I placed my heart with her.

—Who's she?

—She was a college student, she rejected me. I chased after her for years to no avail. I will sue her in court for sexual harassment.

He cracked up as did I. He was intoxicated with joy: "I told you, I have a golden sense of humor."

—I know, I know. What's her name?

—Amanda. The A dances aboard my ship and sings, Amanda. The M dances aboard my ship and sings, Amanda. The N dances aboard my ship and sings, Amanda. The D dances aboard my ship and sings, Amanda. Then the A, the coda, dances aboard my ship and sings, Amanda, Amanda.

—Were you a sailor once, in the blue and foam of the sea?

—Yes. But as the saying goes, no one's totally worthless, even as a bad example. And as an example of bad people she got to know in her life, I am her servant.

I laughed so hard I almost fell off my chair.

—What about your life when she was in it?

—Man, it's not often that I look into my life this way, but when I do, I say, Bari, it's the same old thing they call life.

He stared into space for a bit, then continued.

—I will write a book about my life and call it "The Wrong Journey."

—Why don't you write it?

—Because I live.

I left his apartment after midnight, walked under the streetlights, danced with tree shadows on the asphalt, I was consumed by the stories of the tiger and Amanda, when a fancy red car pulled up to me and startled me with Rock 'n' Roll. I knew no one and wanted to know no one from that class.

A beautiful woman peeked out the car window. She had a small face, big blond hair, golden necklace that circled her breasts, the chains seemed so heavy they could break her frail neck: "Come in, honey," she said and flipped her hair as she embellished a smile.

—How do you know me?

—I don't.

—Where are you from?

—Bellevue. (A wealthy neighborhood.)

I got suspicious. She kept motioning to me to get in. Her voice was strange. Then it occurred to me that she might be a man, and her hair a wig, but it was impossible for me to tell for sure.

—Are you a natural woman?

—Yes, honey.

—Do you feel lonely?

—Who doesn't feel lonely, sweetie?

I would have forgotten about that encounter had the following not happened two days later in Last Exit. In the pocket of his Marines jacket, Bari kept a torn book without a cover. A book whose edges had been burnt and put out with water. Bari smoked and drank coffee as I flipped through the book which appeared to be written by a plastic surgeon in New York interested in Cybernetics. He argued that some clients came to him for surgery on their already beautiful noses that needed no reconstruction. He concluded that cosmetic surgery alone, with scalpel, chemicals, and dissection, did not suffice. One had to understand the mind that imagined its nose in need of beautification.

My mind went back to that queer man in the fancy red car two nights before: to the extent with which a man is able to sense himself as a woman. I encountered many people like that in the United States, men who'd changed their hair, dress, movement, the way they talked, men who imposed on themselves rigorous diet regimens, did all they could to become women. It's almost impossible to tell them apart from women. Some underwent surgery to change their sex. All of them saw a different body in their mind, a feminine body, and did what they could to reconfigure the physical body to match their mental image of it.

My graduate research looked into suicide in novel and drama. It was part of my interest in "How the creative mind works," or "The modes of mind through history." I linked the two: the suicidal mind and the queer mind. The former resembles a timebomb. Whoever engineered the suicidal mind placed a command in it to self-detonate at a given moment. The queer mind "redesigns" the body instead of exploding it.

The mind has a particular design? Isn't this the case with other entities in the universe? This idea would upend my life. The mind is an entity capable of redesigning itself and its world.

I set the tattered book aside and asked Bari: "What's the mind?" "A recorder," he said, "Everything that comes along and passes through you is recorded in it."

—But it isn't a negativism, is it? Children build sandcastles and also demolish them.

—Exactly. You can see the mind as an adaptive entity.

I thought of the words for a while, then added: "I think the mind is also an expansive entity. Let's assume the Babylonians learned something new from building the Tower. Their mind recorded this new knowledge. Doesn't this mean their mind expanded, enlarged? Heraclitus said, 'The logos is a widening cistern.' "

I was animated, looking for another word, not "discover" or "widen," not "adapt" or "record." Create: that's the word. A human's deepest need is to create. I think I read something like that in an ancient sacred text of the East: the enlightened mind is like a candle that transfers its light to other candles without diminishment of its own light.

There's no inspiration in a candle that gives its light over to another candle. A mind that only copies or preserves is likely to suffer paralysis. It loses its essence: to create, to become. The current crisis of the Arab mind is that it has lost its capacity to create. I don't only mean the creation of its world, the formulation of the life it lives, but also the "redesigning" of itself: the mind's capacity to offer something new to itself every night. This is more important. Any mind that has lost its capacity to design itself will be designed by another. I called this ability to reformulate a self, "high geometry," and wrote about it in my poem, "Eastern Jazz":

> I threw my love to the rising tide,
> my hands ebbed with the past.
> The tigers I wrestled in the jungle wounded me,
> and when alone my steps walked over me.
> I wasn't a shepherd of geese or goats
> in your mountains and I wasn't a flute.
> I was the emptiness inside the flute
> without which you cannot sing.
> Where's that emptiness now and where are you?
> My geometry is to design myself.
> My silence croons.

That night I walked for hours in the forest. The vision of the falcon returned: under a blue sky, I was a soaring falcon, flying sideways at high speed. He could see the whole of my memory's geography, a geography I would redesign. The falcon spotted me on the forest trails. We stared at each other a bit. He contemplated me, then continued his flight toward what I haven't yet become: an artist of self-reconfiguration.

In those days I was reading, for the tenth time, Marx's *Capital*. I went to Bari's house at night. He noticed the book as we sat in the living room: "Man, life is not a German logical construction. I swear to God one day I will write a book on what ideologies do to minds."

—Have you read Marx?

—Yes.

—What did you think of him?

—Not of him. Knowledge is impersonal.

—Fine. Of what he wrote?

—He wrote riddles. I studied them for four years.

—Did you solve the riddles?

—I learned something from him: not to lose my sense of the ordinary things and the strange worlds that my soul moves through. That's useful. I mean, don't lose your ordinary sense of the world, Hussein.

—And what are those strange worlds you move through: Where are you now?

—No point in what you can't sense.

—I mean, how does my world appear to you?

—I know nothing about you. The sea depth knows nothing of its shores. Your face is a shore.

That sentence "your face is a shore" shook me. I imagined myself at the bottom of the sea, looking toward the shore, my face. Another thought struck me like lightning. In Beirut, the sea would begin its chase in my dream when I was just a child, sitting naked on a rock on the sandy shore, my clothes in my hand, staring at the sea in fear and amazement. I used to see the sea with the eyes of a child. Never did I try to see the child with the eyes of the sea. I used to see the sea as awesome, stunning, its blue and waves, its schizophrenia and sands, its change of direction as it chased me, but I never saw how the sea saw me. "Your face is a shore." Finally, I could see the child with the sea's eyes.

I imagined myself a sea: in my far distances, a vast blue fog contained lost boats and waves that rose like horses of spume, thrashing brilliantly in all directions. But this whole formulation was foolish: Why would a majestic powerful sea convince itself to chase a dreaming child smaller than a red doll on its shore, a shrunken, naked child holding his clothes and fear of drowning? What would convince a grand force of the universe to chase him?

I was on the threshold of a trance. As if I'd hypnotized myself. "Bari," I said, "for years, the sea used to chase me and my face was a shore."

—Probe its intentions.

—I am. I am staring at myself with the eyes of the sea. My physical body has disappeared, and the sea has become my body. I'm moving through it as a soul in an expanse. I am not a fish in it, Bari, I am the sea.

—Probe its intentions.

Suddenly I started to rise. And the blue rose and swelled, and bit by bit, my enraged waves rose in my depths, from my abdomen and pits, as if I were pregnant with a hoard of snakes and evils that crashed back into the waves, then bloated the belly some more and elevated the blue higher: the deluge began, and Beirut was a doll.

—Probe its intentions, Hussein, probe them.

—All this repressed anger, the deluge, the desire to destroy the world, the insanity, while my center remained blue, sunny, spacious. And all this surface while beneath it I was with enough evils to make my mother wish she'd never given birth to me. Do you know what exile means, Bari, do you know it? This fragile little boy, his red doll, and inside his belly a sea and repressed floods.

—Probe the boy's intentions, Hussein, probe them.

—The sea tempts the boy to meet himself in it, to meet his rage that gods, demons, and past centuries have decreed. How does a sea convince itself to chase a boy? And to what extent did the boy need safety, security? Oh my God, how much force was necessary so that people could bite his heart and create an entire sea of anger in a child's belly? They raped me through to my heart, Bari? You'd said it once to me about you. They raped me until they reached my heart, and I am your brother.

I cried and cried and could no longer remember what happened after those last words. I exited one crying spell to enter another.

Bari said, "Your tears are the final form of the deluge. The sea now overflows out of you in the form of tears." He then stood up and started clapping, singing, chanting, as he circled me: "The mountain boy in you has been acquainted with the sea inside you and they are now one. And you have widened. Blessed be those who widen."

I realized that my fear of becoming schizophrenic, wherein my other self would commit a crime my first self wouldn't know about, was nothing more than my sense of the sea inside me, the waves in which all my destructive desires had dissolved like salt. I was afraid of a split because I was already split. The sea used to chase me because it was the deepest, widest, and most truthful form my anger had known. And its intentions were to destroy the entire world.

—The mountain boy on the seashore is a small lit candle at night, Bari. It is the sea's need for security. And the sea is the candle's desire to transform the universe into dry wood to start the great fire. The result is a boy as tumultuous as the sea and a sea as anxious as a child.

I began to see madness. Anyone who sees such depths is justified to redesign themselves.

And the rage is white.
And she has her rose, that lady
to whom we'll give the universe.
I was a well,
and it's within a well's rights
to become a ladder,
so let's give her the universe.

I was still flooding with sea when I asked Bari, "What is madness?"

—To not recognize your intentions insofar as they're intentions.

—I don't get it. Beirut's sea used to chase me in my dream, for years, man, how do I understand that?

—My mind is a golden knife that I have blunted while trying to help you see yourself.

—But you speak in riddles. What does it mean to recognize my intentions as intentions?

—It means that your anger at the world, your urge to destroy, your fear of drowning to death, your need for safety and security, are only your heart's intentions. But your mind doesn't recognize or comprehend those intentions. This thing you call your mind understands nothing. Your heart has squeezed itself like a large bitter fruit, and all its bitterness it poured into the sea, dissolved in it like salt until the sea is turned bitter. And here comes the flood: your heart is trying to come to you, feed you its black fruit, wants you to feel it, chases you to give you the sea and say to you: This salt and bitter taste is my feeling of life and the summary of yours!

—And what is madness?

—Your heart comes to you disguised as a sea, but you think your heart is Beirut's sea. There are two seas: Beirut's and your heart's. The first is real, the second is the sea of your intentions. And you're ignorant of the difference between the two seas, which is an ignorance of your intentions insofar as they're intentions. It's crazy, man.

—And what's the guarantee against madness?

He went silent again, rolled another of his cigarettes and spit the loose tobacco until the silence became the heaviest I'd known, then he said: "The guarantee against madness is to intend nothing."

I paced his living room back and forth. I was crying, mumbling, "This is unbelievable, simply unbelievable." I had seen the sea, literally, in my belly, seen its blue depths flow toward me, but I couldn't imagine the conclusion: "The sea begins in my belly and ends where? On Italy's shores? I'm unable to bear a belly this big. And blue: is blue the color of my intentions?"

> The boy's a candle,
> security is what he needs.
> And the sea
> is tears
> whose borders are shores
> to which we will
> offer a rose
> and the entire place.

CHAPTER THREE

I met a Mary, a product of Jesuit rearing, a philosopher and a writer of brilliant short stories who published nothing. "I am a famous unknown writer," she said as we sat on the ledge of her window one night, keeping watch over the ocean's rumble. "Hussein," she said, "a person who doesn't offer me knowledge, or expand my comprehension, and doesn't get the same from me is a person I have no use for." She was rocking in a wicker chair and staring into the ocean's roll: "I was friends with a Japanese man once," she added, "and he used to sit in this same spot and mumble: Let's concentrate, let's concentrate, let's concentrate."

A strange blonde woman she was. The last I saw of her, she was with Indigenous Americans learning to become a medicine woman who danced to the moon. Mary, I need you, I want to dance with you to the moon when necessary. I am a simple person, often misunderstood, and that's mostly why I exist in the margins of life and language, and I don't want you to misunderstand me as well.

During my childhood, I used to walk on the prairies, and in my hand an orange wooden cylinder we call a pencil. I'd mumble "pencil, pencil, pencil," without connecting the word to the object. Words appeared to me as acts of magic, wandering amorphous souls that hover above things, like the Lord's soul over water. The first time I encountered "Britannia," for example, in Beirut, was in a military magazine that a man from Tripoli had handed to me. The music of the letters bewitched me, especially that of the first "i" and the second "a." I was further entranced by how the word itself, despite its music, held no meaning for me in those young days—as if the word were proof that there was no autonomous relation between names and things. I called those types of words, closed words, and loved them the most. I started to memorize a lot of foreign names (like "Cinema Carmen") because they came across as sealed. I evolved a special memory of foreign things that were closed up to my soul on first encounter.

I used to walk the mountains of Ramallah toward the springs under summer's blue sky, in the dust of noon, and with my fingertips I'd write my name on the blue above, then take a few steps back to examine "Hussein" in the distance. Sometimes it would appear tilted like a painting on a wall. I'd straighten it or adjust the blue frame or leave the name off balance, and walk on. I'd walk and whisper my name's letters as if I were a student of the great Sufi Ibn Arabi who said, "Letters are nations, and with each letter a nation of jinn can be conjured." I used to hear the jinn whistle in each letter of my name. Words perplexed me, those glassy crystals of colored air.

My relatives noticed the boy who wrote with his fingertips on the blue horizon, the child who talked to himself: they nicknamed me "the fool" or "hatchling fool." The magical power a name wields over the named is immense. The question is not whether there was a "thing" or a "person" that my relatives called a "fool," no, on the contrary, a "fool" was created inside the real Hussein, a foolish identity. And I became what they insinuated I was. The fool already existed inside the word, entered my ears and, from there, coursed to my heart, woke up in the body of my consciousness as an intruder dispatched by other intruders to my world. Black magic? Maybe. I'm not sure. Just recently I started to research the meaning of the word "fool," "Ahbal" in Arabic.

Ahbal is not an Arabic word. It is derived from the name of the pre-Islamic moon god "Hubal." One of its meanings in Aramaic is "smoke." Lunar smoke is my father, yes, my real father. Hussein is no more the true son of this earth, not even the son of his biological father (and I am not spreading rumors here). I am just explaining how Hussein the stranger was born in the form of not one but a congregation of fools and strangers who, despite it all, possess their own private wisdom.

Every Eid, I'd sneak out at dawn to roam the mountains until nightfall. I wanted to see no one and daydreamed of a special invisibility hat that could disappear me if I ran into others, so I'd be neither seen nor heard. But I would be able to see all of them in the yellow-red light of their kerosene lamps as I sat in the far corner of their caves, fully sentient, and could even smell their wives' sweat. I preferred to bury myself in a hat than to be with people. Black magic? Maybe, maybe. Please understand me: the invisibility hat is the dream of cowards. Maybe I was a coward, why not? I'm not ashamed of it. Who isn't a coward for one reason or another. What could a boy do to protect himself in the presence of more powerful elders but become a coward? I became "another," no longer me. And they were no longer themselves, not the men or the women. And "we" lost its meaning.

—You suffer from a sense of lack, a deficiency, I think.

—I feel deficient before the desert not before people.

—Wow, wow, man.

And they gave me another nickname for another foolish identity: "Bucket." There's no limit to the capacity of biting experts. Sorcerers. And little Hussein had access only to Moses's stick. I could toss it and turn it into a snake that swallowed their snakes. This actually happened (the new nickname happened) when my dad came back from Beirut to visit us, and our relatives came to greet him. One of the relatives was a blind imam who had memorized a great deal of classical Arabic poetry and used to sniff from a brown metal container he kept in his pocket. Dad thought he was a wise man. The snuff left a yellow-red stain on his mustache. Dad asked this wise figure his opinion of me. The sniffing imam shook his head right and left and said, "Abu Hussein, your son is a bucket!" I was a child. I fixed my gaze toward him to examine his seriousness. He believed more in my idiocy than Moses believed in God when the latter spoke to him from the right side of the mountain. I was a bucket. "Ahbal." Period. No proof or dialectic could displace an atom of this "mystic" knowledge of the blind imam.

And my dad, like most Palestinian fathers of the time, was a god of silence. He suppressed his rage against his "bucket" son until midnight. Then he woke me up and said, "Take the mule to the spring. And let her drink."

— Our mule had honey eyes, a huge torso, and was tied in a storage room behind a metal door. Scared, half-asleep, barefoot, I led her from her reins and went to the mountains on silent moonlit trails far from humans and homes, and heard a ringing music in the absolute wilderness, bells in the hands of some jinn or ghoul on nearby olive branches where a sense of the world's madness ran through the shadows on the ground. Trembling I stood by a water pool near a big rock as the mule drank. To distract my fear, I alternated between looking at the olive's moonlit shadows and into the mule's honey eyes and long lashes. The water the mule lapped was bubbling. I remembered the story of Jbaineh: she was white as cheese, hence her name. She climbed up a doum palm to pick its fruit and toss it to her friends to put in their leather sacs. She was the most beautiful among them and they were jealous, so they gathered scorpions, grasshoppers, beetles, and pebbles into her sac. They left her up in the tree and headed home. Jbaineh forgot about time. The moon rose and a jinn, Sidi of the Two Horns, arrived and said, "I smell a human on my tree." He spotted her, ordered her to jump down on one of his horns. She landed on the left one. He thought about eating her but changed his mind and took her back to his realm as a shepherdess for his sheep in the thorn-covered mountains. There she sang alone:

> Oh birds flying over high mountains
> tell Mom and tell Dad,
> Jbaineh, shepherdess of geese, struts
> then naps under a grape trellis.

I imagined the ghoul would come catch me. He'd smell a human boy near his water pool. God would protect me, God would. But what if God had created this universe and forgot to create me, this "hatchling fool," what does it matter if God forgot any of his creatures? Unanswerable questions possessed me that night. What if God forgot all his creatures in the universe and created me alone? The questions descended heavier: What if God didn't exist? Later at home I asked Dad and the snuff-sniffing imam about these questions. Any doubts anyone had about my foolishness, my bucket self, were confirmed. "The air blew, fool, follow the air, fool." And when I avoided their songs, they labeled me "deaf." My dad was hard of hearing, especially as he got older, and the mockery was meant for us both. The world of sound was no longer mine. I was abandoned. I grew closer to the moon: a sheer eye of smoke. Simply put, these events destroyed my sense of hearing.

—Wow, wow, man. Words are magic, and the clan is bound together in the heart, and when these heart bonds are slackened, the clan is loosened. And your heart paid the price.

—What about you?

—I'm an individual, man, I have no origin and no branch.

—True. The clan was bound together in the heart, and I was outside that bond. From time to time I'd lose my consciousness, yes, my consciousness. Once, at the house of a man in the clan, they were all laughing at me and I stared at their faces, they were nothing more than strange open mouths like caves painted red. Flesh caves of odd architecture. And the words they spoke and interrupted each other with dissolved into a current of meaningless sounds, a foreign language. I left that house and didn't recognize the road, the neighborhoods, not even the trees.

—That's the internal magnet. When the rust of consciousness is attracted to the internal magnet, you can't recognize your exterior.

—And then during my last year in high school they nicknamed me "genius." They were serious. From "hatchling fool" to "genius," without transition.

Their surprise was because I'd written a poem for some school contest in the Ramallah district. No one believed I was the author, not the professors at Birzeit, not the judges, or my teacher. They accused me of stealing it from some "major poet." And they held a tribunal for me. The news spread. I became known as "the genius." It was less important that I was a hatchling fool, deaf, or genius than that I was always outside the context: odd and strange, on the margin of the world, I belonged to no one. A genius without prologue. Do you understand me: this is just a word. In my personal history, this word holds no good intentions. And in its personal history as a word, it holds no good intentions either.

Pre-Islamic Arabs believed in invisible, concealed creatures, jinn that move from one place to another with a wink, a blink of the eye. Some of them resided in Wadi 'Abkar (the root for the Arabic word for "genius"): a place no one could place. In this non-place, Arabs believed that the jinn residents are those who transmit poetry to poets, and thus a poet is called 'abkari, a genius mysteriously connected to Wadi 'Abkar. This Wadi is alluded to in the Quran when it declared that poets "wander in the wadi." Calling me a genius placed me on the threshold between human and jinn, between mind and madness. The word was not a recognition of who I am. It was a distancing of the hatchling fool to prairies of greater weirdness.

I began to delete human voices from my world. What else could a boy like me do? My love focused on the mountains and on matter, not people. Prairies became my companions. Stone, ears of wheat, birds, and whatever else that crossed my path became my interlocutors. One time I held court between two wheat spikes, and my verdict was that one should wilt. Under the shade of olive trees, I played with stone dolls. I befriended a sparrow, then a dog. And finally I stumbled upon friends for the road: words. I toiled in and flowed into *A Thousand and One Nights*, the *Mu'allaqat*, words and things were my friends, but not people. Words are elevators, by the way. Each word is an elevator.

By the late Sixties in Beirut, I saw my first elevator. We lived in a building whose entrance was a beautiful mosaic of gypsum and marble. The elevator was golden, had a mirror and buttons. I felt it was a magic closet. I saw an older woman with gold rings who lived on the fourth floor. Um Maroun would enter the magic closet, close the door behind her, and rise. She'd leave me behind, alone. I was confused. Where did she go? I pressed the button, and the closet returned. I opened the door, and she wasn't there, no trace. I was stunned, convinced that whoever entered the closet simply disappeared.

Another time a pleasant young Christian girl rode the closet. She was giggling. As usual I pressed the button to bring the elevator back down and when I opened the door, a white-haired old man appeared carrying a basket with a small white dog in it. It occurred to me that the magic closet converted gender and age: man became woman, woman became man, and the old, young, the young, old. It was futile to disagree with those who enter the magic closet: clearly their desire was to become another, or simply vanish for a while.

I'd sit in front of the elevator door monitoring its passengers, opening the door for them to enter and exit, mesmerized by this incarnation game. Imagine my astonishment when one day I opened the door and Um Maroun herself came out with the same gold rings on her fingers, reincarnated into her original form.

I lost comprehension. For a while I didn't go inside the magic closet or upstairs. I only opened the door for the important people who lived in the building. One such person was a Maronite jeweler. Another worked at the state department in Tripoli. And another was a famous Palestinian writer, Ghassan Kanafani, who was friends with my dad.

Taken by this transforming magic closet, I was keen to open the door to anyone who wanted to disappear or reincarnate. Maybe they thought I was there to serve them. So the residents and passengers started to tip me. As if I had enlisted in the forces of wizardry and sorcery, and got gratuity out of it.

Finally, I decided to take a ride in the magic closet, become a girl, an old man, a government employee, or whatever creature. Inside, I closed the door behind me. Bewildered, I stared into the mirror, at the gilded ceiling and the orange and yellow floral rug, waiting for the miracle to commence. Nothing happened. There was a gilded horizontal metal bar over my head. I swung from it. Suddenly the magic closet started to rise, and I let go of the bar. The closet stopped between two floors. I saw a lattice of black wood and behind it a pale-yellow immovable cement wall. To no avail I tried to push the wall open. I am one of those claustrophobic people. With my two little hands I pushed again. The closet terrified me. I could sense a wild animal's frightened scream growing in me. I kept pushing against the wall. Then I hung from the gilded metal bar again to see what might happen.

The elevator's base rests on spring coils. A person's weight drives it downward when that person operates the button board by the mirror. Hanging from the metal bar a second time released my weight from the base and the closet rose once more and I was saved.

I made it a habit: to enter the closet, swing from the bar, wait, then ascend or descend to anyone who pressed the call button. When the door opened and a client of the magic closet was outside, I felt ecstasy, as if I'd materialized from a magician's sleeves.

The closet was tethered to steel ropes on pulleys propelled by a large engine situated in a room on the roof. I stole the keys and snuck inside that room, started messing with the buttons and dials in it. Some of those gauges interrupted the electrical output and seized the closet. I turned into a prison warden for the closet's clients. The residents thought electricity would spontaneously cut off. I wouldn't simply restore it by the press of a button. Instead I'd operate the manual lever to get the closet to the next floor opening, then rush down to meet the freed client, inform them that I was their savior, and invariably they'd tip me.

Imprisoning others became a source of income for me. This little revenue fount, I kept hidden from my dad. It was the stash I used for going to Cinema Carmen at night, independent of his aid, and it was the stash from which I paid to play pool, or buy a small red plastic jug for my mom. Dad searched the entire house for my cash but couldn't find it. I used to hide it under the floral rug in the magic closet, right under everyone's feet, so to speak, those affluent feet as I took them to be, those clients who will not stoop that low to look for my treasure. Then a group of kids in the building began to refer to me as "that Palestinian," pointing at me, whispering about me. I'd not heard that expression used to describe me before. It was a foreign expression to my ears, another sealed, meaningless word that, as I later found out, came from the name of an ancient people who worshipped fire. Those boys, about fifteen of them, ganged up on me. Monikers are peculiar. All any of those boys needed to do was call me that strange word, "Palestinian," and they'd rush toward me, down the stairs, out of the closet, from the street, circling me in the building's foyer behind their leader, Ali, who was older and bigger than I was.

I was a tough mountain kid, strong built, possessed with stone's cruelty, and I could wrestle the whole gang, place Ali in a headlock with my left arm, drag him into the directions of the kicks his friends launched at me, so they'd hit him instead as I hit them with my right arm. But fifteen is too many, so I thought of another trick. With my under-the-rug budget I bought a black plastic gun, a plastic police baton, and handcuffs: a weaponized gear fitting of a place that can't seem to live without a civil war every now and again. It was a water gun that I filled with salt water. The baton hung on my waist, the handcuffs on my belt, and I waited for them in the foyer while strutting my stuff like a general in his labyrinth.

They attacked. I grabbed Ali's head and dragged him as usual. With the gun in my right hand I sprayed my salt liquid into their eyes. They were in shock and avoided me for quite a while until they came up with a counterplan. Ali grabbed my right wrist and another kid, my left. The gun was useless. It was clear I was headed for total humiliation, so I dragged both kids toward a glass door at the end of the hall and slammed Ali's hand against the glass. It bled. The gang's horrified screams suffused the air. Residents came down. Dad came in from outside the building.

"The Palestinian" was the first of my monikers that bled. I fully realized then, for the first time, how dangerous words can be. Ali and I became friends. He was the first friend to take me to the sea.

A few years after that, the most violent civil war in the history of Lebanon erupted. I visited Beirut to see my childhood. In the marble entrance of that building, another man, not my dad, sat in a wicker chair. And in what used to be our dwelling (as custodians of the building), opposite the entrance, lived another family. "Can I help you?" he asked. "A cup of coffee, perhaps?" he added. I stood contemplating the entrance until a woman carrying a fruit basket came and asked the man who I was. I recognized her: Um Maroun.

"Do you remember me?" She seemed confused before she drifted: "Are you Jameel's son?" she asked. "Yes, I am," I said. Her husband, Abu Maroun, was an alcoholic. He drank Araq nightly in his pistachio-colored pajamas that showed his gray chest hair. He owned a jewelry shop in Burj plaza in Beirut's commercial district. Um Maroun invited me to lunch at her apartment. We went upstairs. I asked about the jewelry shop, she said it was destroyed. I asked about her husband, she said alcohol killed him. I asked about her son, Maroun, and she said he was killed in the war. Nothing was left except a lunch in silence. As for the other residents: the Mossad had assassinated Ghassan Kanafani with a car bomb. Um Maroun said that his remains had been gathered off trees, his wrist watch retrieved from the roof of a nearby building. Still ticking.

What I want to say is that words were one of the reasons for this bloody civil war. Each "sect" had its name or characteristic, and each sect despised whatever moniker another sect called it by, and each sect had their "words" and their way of saying those words. Language is a black magic. Anyhow, after my issues with Ali and the kids of that building, I reverted to my individual world. Outside that world I was always a "dangerous kid" to other kids, a "Palestinian" in their eyes, a stranger to them and their sects.

A human child or a child of jinn: I was solitary, a kid confined to himself, in his private hollow sphere, obsessed with letters, or scared of ghouls, or moonstruck, whatever. The important thing was my heart, and it was alive, fully aware of a charmed world, a spirituality coursing through things and the universe, and whether this spirituality was called jinn, a smokey moon, a riddle, an apparition, idiocy, a folktale, or a hyena, all I can say is that the water wells were possessed, the caves were possessed, and the self was possessed—I was a multitude in others who each had a name, although I did not feel I had one: I was not a genius, not a hatchling fool, not deaf, not Palestinian, or anything else, I was a namelessness personified, a secret sense between me and me. And this "transparent concealment," this creature without a name, this being between "the named" and the "unnamed" is the me who was smitten with the magic of language and sealed words.

Words are like land, divided into spheres of influence. Sharply I distinguished between two spheres separated by a fence: "their words," those experts at snipping and biting, and "my words." I fled to the land of my words, a strange land I'd write, delete, construct, deconstruct, converse with, do with it what I wished instead of a world that did with me as it wished. My words were soft, extremely pliable, shaped by mere touch from a child's finger, or sometimes like the dirt I used to play with, a smooth powder from which a pistachio cascade flows into a bottle, or a kind of bottle in which I imagined palaces, great halls, and transparent roads, though no people, because people were made of stone . . . but no, no, stones and rocks were my friends, too. People, however, I wasn't sure about them: weird creatures one couldn't be certain of their isness. No utterance meant necessarily what it meant when people spoke it. They possessed invisible dimensions like a water well I used to love in the mountains: I'd stare into the well under the moonlight and speak so that an expansive, deep echo would bounce back, an echo they had a name for in the countryside, "Amoureh": a spirit that turns a place alive, populates it with imperceptible force. As with this well, the words that were uttered into people returned to me as an amplified echo, strangers to me donned by other spirits. Oh, Bari, they raped me until they got to my heart, my sorrow was incredible.

—Who of us wasn't raped, my friend. People's mouths are one well after another.

There was such a well in our village inside a Roman cave: "Sitti Ain el-Qubah" (Our Lady Well of the Dome). At the cave's entrance stood a huge oak. At any time, any passerby with any negative thought in their mind, or if they took a piss or crossed an invisible boundary of some kind, had to tie a black or yellow ribbon, or a strip from their clothes to a branch of that oak. If they didn't, Our Lady would visit them in their dreams and kidnap them to another world. The legend was that the well would flood from time to time and could drown the neighboring mountains if it wanted to. Then after "seven lean years" the well went dry. "She will overflow soon," they said, "if we offer her a young girl, a sacrifice." But no one offered their girl. To my mind, people were like Our Lady. I offered them no daughter and no sacrifice to help their love to overflow. Little did I know in those days that I, too, would dry up in secret, as Our Lady did, and would receive no offers to help me to overflow.

I was alive, receding, inhabited by various spirits. Yet even this dearth I eventually lost. An anxious drought took over my soul. I began to lose my heart. My madness arrived at the maqam of sand—which reminds me of a sacred river forest for Indigenous Americans that "White progress" had annihilated into environmental rubble of absent waters and dead trees: they asked an old Indigenous warrior about the secret of this destruction. He said: "I don't know. All the waters and forests used to be populated with spirits and gods but now they all died, or were annihilated, or they emigrated." That's what's become of me: the soul of forest and water died in my heart or emigrated or was annihilated, I'm not sure.

Heart drought! That's all it was. My mind was growing as my heart was drying up. The magical consciousness I grew up with, as did other Palestinian villagers, was invaded by "modern scientific knowledge," that cold, precise, "objectivity." I became like Mustafa Saeed in *Season of Migration to the North*. What died inside me was dead, and the heart went dry.

Out of this pain and desiccation I started to write songs. As I got older, I transformed Jbaineh's folksong (the one I recalled as I led the reddish mule to the water spring) into lyrics for a band that played it for thousands of people at the Palestine Festival in Birzeit. The audience's response surpassed my expectation. Far from the crowd, I sat on a wall and observed. The depth of singing sometimes comes from the depth of pain, just as golden laughter sometimes comes out of innumerable mazes. I wrote a lot of songs, and still my heart gradually dried. In 1985, my condition reached surreal levels. I became insensate. Everything stopped. There was no hint of soul in words. I decided to learn how to play the flute. Imagine: a flute player in that ancient hell.

By the end of 1985, I rented a house with a glass terrace surrounded by a rose garden. The house was on the border between the Arab Jerusalem and the Jewish one, as if it were a zone of sin. Opposite it was an old, large Palestinian house rimmed by big pine trees, wrapped with a dilapidated fence wire. The energy of that ruin drew me to it. I felt a resemblance between us, and so I started composing music while staring at it. At night, countless dogs barked from the place, barked and barked, madly and furiously, as if something was going on inside the house, inside the dogs, or inside me. The yellow-lit streets were empty, there was no one who could hear what I was hearing. All I saw were shut windows, once and forever, they seemed to be eternally shut on families or on brothels or whatever would not reveal itself. I tried to play my music, but the barking drowned my tune, so I put down the flute and wandered in my thoughts about that place. Places are like people, they hide their suspicions and fears, possess their private lexicon and logic.

One night, almost naked, I stood in the terrace with the lights off, staring at that barking-filled house, when an old, kyphotic woman with white and uncombed hair came out. She was wearing a light-colored linen nightgown, a dirty pink almost, and her breasts sagged. In her right hand was a black trash bag. She went up the vacant road with yellow lights, talking to herself. Her appearance insinuated a world that had been destroyed centuries ago, a world populated with dogs that bark in the lonely madness.

I dozed off in a spacious room that overlooked the rose garden with a mysterious apprehension in my heart. The savage barking woke me after midnight. It was particularly sharp as if an insane person were flogging the dogs with aluminum wires, tearing apart the animals who, in turn, tore into his flesh. I heard the woman screaming. Unconsciously I presumed the criminally insane person was raping her, exterminating her, or flogging her along with the dogs, so I ran past the glass doors, out on the terrace, through the garden, to the street. Under the yellow lights she stood shaking her fist at the heavens for some reason and shouting in Hungarian. It shocked me that she was a Hungarian Jew, perhaps from an aristocratic family before Communism took hold, or a survivor of the Nazis in World War II, and that she was living in a traditional Palestinian house, perhaps renting it from its owners, since the house was in the border zone, or that she simply possessed the house after its Arab residents had been expelled from it as usual.

I shouted in her direction in Hungarian: "What's going on?" She switched her fist toward me and intensified the pumping, headed my way in revolt as if I were the source of her dogs' tragedy. And then it hit me: I was in my underwear, almost naked. Horrified, I glanced at the windows in the street. I would be accused of raping her. What else could it mean that I was standing almost naked after midnight in a prohibited zone? The province of the night in Jerusalem was prohibited to all Palestinians from "the occupied territories" without a military permit, which I did not have. They'd accuse me of attempting to rape an old Jewish woman while breaking their laws that prohibit movement, the former a civil case, the latter a military court. The windows were shut and lit. I was terrified. Did anyone see me? I ran back to the terrace and closed the glass door behind me. I was trembling: even sympathy for others had become dangerous.

Not long after this incident I arrived in Seattle. I began to wander in the night in the woods on campus, lost in thought after thought in some horizon, some poem, some philosophy, but neither my heart felt what I thought, nor my mind ceased to dominate my soul. Each idea turned into a piece of petrified wood, period.

My wandering attracted the attention of the American police who set up a trap for me: a woman inside a yellow cab. She reminded me of that Hungarian woman, though this one was peacefully asleep with the door open. The idea was that I was a rapist looking for prey, and that a sleeping woman would excite the dogs of my instincts to attack. Smart, the police: my intentions were sexual, no doubt. The madness on whose door I stood offered me one solution only: desire devoid of beauty. But rape was never on my mind, and the police were stupid: I desired a woman, not a ghost.

Anyway, I'd stroll until daybreak, lost in thought after thought as I said until, exhausted, my head would stop moving and I'd turn toward contemplating other things: neon lights, police traps, trash bins, etc.

One time I spotted a penny in the street, picked it up, mindlessly put it in my pocket, just a useless whim. Gradually I started collecting pennies. I'd spot their glare a mile away. I turned into a cat spotting a copper mouse. In my studio apartment, I collected the pennies in a jar and daily counted them. I grew addicted to collecting pennies or trash (as Don was). But pennies were not that ubiquitous, not many people tossed them away in those days, or if they did, many other wanderers like me got to them first.

Aimless walking was an impossibility. I turned to collecting soda cans for months.

And out of one addiction grew another. I remembered how Gogol, who went mad as a young man, would suffer bouts of depression and invent hilarious scenarios so that he might laugh, just to laugh and survive his depression. Inspired by this invented satire, he wrote short stories. Gogol was quite moved by puppetry. He saw a puppet inside each person or, more precisely, a caricature in each human. And I saw the caricature in me: a graduate student of world literature collecting pennies and soda cans.

My obsession shifted: based on this illogical absurdity, I decided to write short stories full of satire so that I might laugh. I managed a collection to entertain my queer and vagabond friends at Last Exit. All this was before I met you, Bari.

Here's one of those stories.

The Story of the Rock:

I received a real rock in the mail. One cubic meter of stone. "Incredulous." A post-office slip from East Jerusalem said I had a package. When I got there, I was told by the staff that it would cost me twenty thousand dollars. "Say what?" Yes: one dollar plus another plus another to twenty thousand. I thought about walking away from this clowning around, but it occurred to me that the cost likely indicated an extraordinary content. I sold our house in the refugee camp, borrowed six dollars from my paternal uncle, five from a maternal one, sold my books, etc., until I gathered the whole amount and received the rock. At first, I couldn't believe my eyes: a rock! stamped from various countries. It looked like the rock's journey began at the Sydney port and from there to Marseille's port then to Pearl Harbor and on and on. For half a century, the rock had been going around ports and crossing borders until, at last, it reached the port of Haifa and then the post office in Jerusalem, colorfully tattooed with stamps and stickers.

For this I'd sold everything I owned. I put my mother and younger brother up in a cheap motel in Old Jerusalem as I waited for God's help. I still had to pay porters to deliver the rock to the motel. I wasn't crazy to leave it at the post office after all that money I spent. The rock stayed in a corner in the cheap motel room. The motel was so cheap it would get less than one star, a decimal of one. It had no water, running or still, hot or cold. "Incredulous, I mean, really," my mom said as I sat in front of the rock, thinking. "We ended up in a motel because of your rock and your brain," she said, "and your brother can't go to school because of your rock?" For my mom, this was not "our" rock but mine alone.

In 1948, an uncle of mine travelled to the US and didn't come back. The rumor was that he owned bars in Las Vegas, never married. I thought that maybe in his old age he sent the rock to check if he had any heirs. I rang him. He said he'd never heard of me or my birth and he would sue me if I ever contacted him again. Then I thought the rock had an archaeological value of some kind. I sent a piece of it to the Hebrew University. The result came a week later: worthless. With one dollar, they said, you can purchase a cubic mile of this kind of rock.

Due to its entertainment quality, the story reached the media. Wherever I went people asked me: "How's the rock doing?" I found a remote small cafe in the suburbs of West Jerusalem where no one would know me. I needed to contemplate the situation of the rock. I ordered Arabic coffee from the thin, blonde Jewish Russian waitress. She served me the coffee and said, "It's on the house. How's the rock doing?"

As a last resort, I thought of renting a car to take the rock to a mountaintop and roll it down to the wadi. I was conflicted because of my guilt. I made my family suffer in a cheap motel over a rock that I rolled down a mountain. As a compromise I made a promise to myself that I'd never forget the finale: how I rolled the rock, how it rolled—all of it would dwell in my memory. But my perseveration increased. I started to have nightmares about the rock, and I had to draw the line.

No more nightmares. I bought paint and painted the rock with bright colors, orange, yellow, red and whatever might please an onlooker. I wanted to feel happiness when I looked at it myself. Instead, I dreamt that I was in a vast moonlit valley full of colored rocks, rose, yellow, red, etc., and I was running among the rocks like an orphaned child calling for his mother. Then another dream: a rock the size of half the Earth on my head, and me, as if a compressed sponge, breathless. Then another dream and so on and so forth. How do I get rid of the rock? At last, I found a solution: I decided to worship it. I bought two candles, placed them before the rock, lit them at night, surrounded the rock with wine chalices, and put the mail slip on top of the rock. Piously and quaveringly, I spent hours every night in that spot. The rock clearly possessed a mysterious force beyond anyone's capacity to comprehend.

A tourist guide friend of mine came to visit me. The minute he spotted me, he laughed so hard he fell into pieces. He came because he'd heard of my story but didn't expect I'd reached the point of worshipping a rock. I suggested to him that he should bring his tourists to my cheap motel. "Why?" he asked. "I'll tell you why: I will write a fabricated history of the rock, that it was holy during Canaanite times before the Romans seized it in some BCE year. Eventually, the rock was lost until a bedouin stumbled on it during the Crusades. Let me work out the details, and we will publish them in a handsome, gilded booklet that draws tourists to the rock, and we will split the profit." He gave it a long think then, suddenly, as if out of a trance, said: "Deal."

For a month I buried myself in books at the Hebrew University library. I completed a brochure in which I paid attention to the accuracy of events in time and place, fortified with quotations from the works of various historians. And off to the printers. In no time, everything was set on a new path. I made back all the money I'd lost, signed a contract with a Swiss publisher to turn the brochure of the rock into a book, and from one project into another I went. But one night deep into this magnificent game, the police came and surrounded the motel. A fat officer spoke: "You're under arrest. And the rock, as you know, belongs to the state, as do all relics and finds. You have broken the law." I was cornered so I bargained: "I'll give you the rock, but let me keep the money. Otherwise it will be a public scandal in the papers that will tarnish the state's reputation and damage tourism."

We made a deal. The police took the rock to a museum of antiquities in Jerusalem near Hebron's Gate, and the years rolled on. One day I was passing by the museum. A long line of tourists stood waiting to see "the rock," and in each tourist's hand was the brochure I'd written. I laughed and kept on moving but after a few steps, I stopped and said to myself: "I swear to God this rock possesses a secret." I went back, grabbed a brochure, stood in line to see the rock.

Stories of this kind. I thought of several of them when I remembered that Gogol, before he went mad, would suffer bouts of horrible depression and invent humorous situations to entertain himself and then compose them. I was trying to learn from some of this universal history of madness.

—Your heart is suffocating, man, suffocating.

What Bari meant was that life without a heart or with a suffocated heart is fraudulent. But I didn't comprehend that then. All that they taught me in college about objective thought is just another name for this fraud, another rock in an academic mail. We were talking at Last Exit that evening. There was a blonde waitress with a white apron and a face dry as caulk, totally sealed, she didn't smile or make pleasantries as she lit the kerosene lamps on the tables. Bari was staring at her, smoking his cigarette in silence. I asked him: "What do you call someone like me who thinks and thinks and thinks but doesn't feel what he's thinking, needs a pine branch to prop up books on his shelf, and lives in his head, as Suzan said?"

He turned to me, his eyes widening with the madness of one horrified at what he'd just seen: "That's called a deficiency in the filling of your soul, in your core."

—I think . . .

—Don't think, just understand. When the mind possesses the heart, the heart dries up. You're dry, man.

—And what is dryness?

—A type of fakeness.

—Am I a fake?

—Yes!

I turned my gaze to the kerosene lamps, suppressed my contempt, spoke softly so that I didn't disturb another young blonde woman playing the piano: "Here I am at Last Exit, weighing seventy kilos, in a corner all my own, no different than tables and lamps. This much is a fact, and as true as any truth should be respected, because truth exists. So what does it mean that I am a fake truth?"

—You're so thorny, I don't know how to grab a hold of you.

—I'm a fraud, phony, but what makes a thing fake?

—Anything the heart sets aside and says: this is fake. Your heart, not I, set all your life aside and said: this is fake.

—I'm fake? What about you? Everyone here thinks you're psycho or schizophrenic.

—I'm sick, at least. I recover and only the ill recover. But you, you're a hopeless case, not even sick. Fakeness is a truth whose existence negates it.

That precision amazed me. A fake person as I am doesn't need another person or any proof to negate my existence. I am the ultimate proof against myself. My pain at seeing this in myself was unbearable. It's not easy to see the truth, especially one's truth. Choked, I spoke: "Bari, can you teach me something without destroying me? You claw at the worst in me."

—Hussein, I don't destroy when I point to a previous destruction. No pain, no gain.

—What do you mean?

—Take mental retardation, for example.

—OK.

—There is retardation of the heart as well. Your heart is retarded, period. Let your heart grow, man.

One sign of a retarded heart is this feeling of guilt that used to ambush me, a state that turns consciousness into a court of law with judges, lawyers, police, allegations, and a defendant. My heart was a setup of that kind, like in Kafka's *Trial*.

—Who are they, those who live in our heads and accuse us, Bari?

—I don't know, man.

—OK. What is guilt?

He rolled another Osman tobacco cigarette, and stared away for a bit: "Guilt is the effect of a heart that has not yet learned to live with its own effect."

—Example?

—Prince Hamlet.

In those days, I had a recurring dream: standing under a full moon in a small cemetery at the edge of the village where I was born in Palestine, and the mountains around me swimming in silence. I was naked. A soft red velvet scarf covered all but my shoulders as I spoke to the dead: "I am not prince Hamlet, nor was meant to be." A line by T. S. Eliot.

Hamlet is hesitant, incapable of real and decisive action to avenge his father. The secret of this paralysis is his crushing guilt, according to Freud. In the dream, I spoke Eliot's words in Arabic. This translation has two possible meanings: I am not meant to be prince Hamlet because I am accused of being Hamlet, or I am not meant to be, to exist at all, that I am a void, less than a ghost. The setting itself, oh my God! Red velvet in a moonlit cemetery! Perhaps I was talking to my father who'd been dead for years.

I told Bari about the dream. He said: "Your heart didn't learn to feel or to live in its feeling except when it turns itself into hell."

I told him that in Arabic the word for heart also means turning or flipping things (upside down, so to speak, an overthrow). And from the same root comes the word for container. The heart fluctuates between being a container and a revolution of the soul. He shook his head with the pleasure of a child who's found something: "That's the partition, the liminal," he said.

Bari spoke the Arabic word for it, "barzakh." And that floored me, that I'd forgotten he was Turkish. We were one culture once upon a time. My dad knew a lot of Turkish words. And we collapsed together with the Turks: the Arabs became colonies for the West, and the Turks became ghosts after Ataturk "westernized" the state. And here we are, Bari and I, children of this wandering history, together in America, able to communicate only in English, having lost our sense of our mutual bonds to the point that I found his familiarity with Arabic strange.

Anyway, it occurred to me that "barzakh" is a partition in the heart between two waters: one salt, the other fresh. And through the gate that separates the two waters, one water overflows into the other. The bitter into the joyous and vice versa.

In the Mediterranean basin, the distinction between salt and fresh water is ancient. In the Quran, a barzakh partitions two seas that God has destined never to meet. I felt as if ecstasy is fresh water in the heart, in the depths detected only by those who are meant to detect them, a sea of positive feelings, like hope and comedy. And there's another sea, salty with fear, pain, regret, sorrow, revenge, jealousy, and other negative feelings. A barzakh sits between the positive and negative seas that meet only when the world becomes brackish, unclear, as when a waterfall delivers itself to a salty sea that dominates it. I call this mixing of the two waters in the heart: overflow. I was certain that my madness was linked to the

overflow of my negative sea in my heart, from which the condition of a dry heart—or as we say in Palestine, a dead heart,
a stone heart, a heartless heart—follows. The state of overflow
has its conditions, stations, and maqamat. In the case of
Majnoon Laila, for example, the heart is drowning in negative
feelings such as being deprived of the beloved, immersed in
loss and banishment of desires. Instead of a dry heart,
Majnoon has a crazy heart.

In the ancient Egyptian sect of Ptah, everything originated
in the heart, like representations that overflow into language
for the tongue to articulate. Even deities were born as representations in the heart. And for the Sumerians, millennia
ago, gods used to get drunk, and that's when it occurred to
them to create humans they could enslave, humans to serve
them food and drink. The first thing the Sumerian gods
created in humans was the heart, then the rest of the body
around it. And in all Sufi schools, the heart comes first, or second, after the soul. In the *Epic of Gilgamesh*, there's no real
meaning of the soul, only of the heart. When Enkidu dreams
that the council of the gods decreed his death, he is asked by
Gilgamesh: "Why does your heart speak to you thus?" That,
too, a medieval Arabic Sufi poet said: "My heart tells me you'll
be my ruin." The underworld in Gilgamesh is "the dream of
the heart," its speech. And as Nietzsche said, we humans first
saw the gods in our dreams.

During my time in the library of secrets, I meticulously
studied a catalog of negative feelings and another of positive
ones. The catalog was in "The Necklace of Clear Understanding," but those lists suggested a frozen hardness. I
preferred the notion of sea for emotion. A sea is closer to a

128

heart's movements. Two seas separated by a barzakh, a neutrality. Indifference is not neutral. And entanglement where there's no entanglement is not neutral either. The Barzakh of Neutrality is a mystery.

The heart is like a transparent piece of glass. One side looks through to the world and the other to the unknown. I asked Bari: "What is the heart?"

—Pure intelligence.

—I'll think about it. Let me think about it, God damn my thinking.

—Don't think. You'll understand it some other way.

Of these "other ways" I thought a lot. Those who appear sane are incapable of keeping their distance from "rationalizing madness." I held on to my mind with maximum force. And my mind is huge, an astonishing metal skeleton, it used to fascinate even my professors in college. But my mind was also leaning like Pisa's tower, heading for a fall, and fall it would, that was its destiny and fate. All this was too certain, fait accompli, a knowing that my heart, my "pure intelligence," sensed. It's charming how seductive madness can be. How it drew me to it, how much I desired it and set my mind on it, "and to each person what they intend." I was metal shavings drawn to a magnetic mountain, a mountain I knew nothing about, a concealed mountain, moonlit in a landscape of quasi madness that recalls something al-Mutanabbi wrote: "Were I man enough to fill my shoes in this wilderness, I'd hear the jinn in their low hideouts croon."

In rationalizing my madness, I turned away from deterministic knowledge of what I already knew was present in my heart—I refused to see it, dared not, or could not, but Bari could, and I wanted to see what he could see, and it was unbearable to me that I couldn't.

Back then, Bari looked to me like a creature with a falcon's head and an oracle's torso, a stone-age priest with a wolf's tail, a woman's breasts, a horse's head, and so on. He was a gathering of the forces of animal instincts.

He was a talisman. And I was like Ali Baba, a prisoner in a cave full of jewels, gold, and grain, locked up behind a rock that opened only to a secret word that I'd forgotten. "Open sesame." And in my madness I'd shout and scream "Open fava, open wheat, open monkey, open . . . " anything but sesame. I became a captive in the cave of the forty thieves, felt every feature of every wall in that cave, saw no exit. But the first time I met Bari, I knew he knew the secret word.

For example, we met once at Grand Illusion Cinema, the whole gang: Bari, Suzan, Don, Wayne, my roommate the Rajneesh follower, his girlfriend from Chicago (who was lost and shaky like a tennis net), and myself. It was a boring get-together. I left them and went back to my studio apartment. Later that night, Don stopped by. I thought he was going to ask me why I had left the group or if he could crash at my place for the night. "Welcome, Don, come in." "No, thank you. I drew this for you," he said, and handed me a folded paper. I examined his painting. He had scribbled a feral foot on the paper with sharp and random lines of red ink. The foot was wrapped in lines to suggest a leather sandal. The toes were grotesque and dirty with dark red spots under the nails as if the foot had crossed seven thousand miles of cane fields riddled with mosquitoes. I felt a deep pain and didn't notice that Don had gone and left me standing at my door.

That night Don spoke to me in a dream: "You with the red footwear, you who's close to fire, you're not alone, you're a member of the green herd." I woke up, jotted down the sentence on an old piece of paper in my pocket, and in the morning headed to Last Exit, groggy and thinking of Don.

As usual Bari came, asked me for a couple of bucks for coffee, sat down and rolled his cigarette, staring at it as he rolled it between his fingers. Before I could read to him what Don had spoken to me in the dream, Bari unfolded a chess board between us and started setting up the pieces. His lips contorted in some kind of disgust. "Be careful, man," he said, "there are people who are jealous of your strength."

—Who?

—Doesn't matter.

—How did you know?

—Doesn't matter.

I didn't get it. Who are those people who are jealous of my strength? And what are these powers that I possess to deserve such jealousy. Maybe something happened after I left the group last night at Grand Illusion, and that's why Don stopped by? Is that why Bari was talking like this?

I went looking for Suzan. I found her that evening at Grand Illusion. "What happened last night, Suzan, after I went home?" "Nothing," she said, "I said that you are smart, and that girl from Chicago said, 'Yes, for sure.' That's all. Why do you ask?"

Oh my! From this one phrase, "Yes, for sure" Bari understood that the woman from Chicago was jealous of me? And there I was, the hatchling fool since my childhood, unaware that I was surrounded by those who were jealous of powers I was not aware that I possessed? From one phrase?

Years after this incident, I watched *Silence of the Lambs*, that movie about a tailor who imagines himself a woman and murders a series of women, then skins them to weave dresses he can wear, to feel he's become a woman who dances to music in dim lights, touches himself erotically, whispers to some mysterious man: "Fuck me, fuck me."

In the film, another criminal, a professor of psychology, explains the serial murderer to a young detective: "You must understand his essence, his core, his soul's pure condensation. As for jealousy, we only feel jealous of those we know. And that tailor of skin suits is jealous of women for being women," the professor says, and adds: "I was surrounded by several of those skin tailors, weavers who stole my energy and depleted my hope until I felt exhausted and depressed. I needed validation, recognition, tenderness, warmth, but they gave none of it and bit my heart. I felt bleak, dry, besieged by variable invisible parasites that stung my soul, and insects that hatched under my skin, insects stranger than those in the Amazon."

From one phrase, Bari understood the most debased energies around me, those skin tailors.

He had a falcon's eyes and an oracle's vision. He was as poor as a temple mouse. And as I write these words, I still don't know how he paid his rent in that "college dorm," inexpensive as it was, a hundred and fifty dollars a month or thereabouts. But he used to borrow money from me every morning for his coffee and say: "I will give you back every dollar, every penny, when I get a job."

After the narrative of jealous skin tailors, I ran into Bari one night. He invited me and Don to dinner. I found the invitation strange. Bari was sad and distracted. I knew something had happened.

We left Last Exit and headed down University Boulevard. The tarmac glistened in the cold neon light. We reached the Safeway and went behind it where the green dumpsters were. Bari pointed to the boxes in the dumpster and spoke: "They throw things good to eat here, come." He ran toward one of the dumpsters and climbed into it, started poking the trash with one hand and smoking with the other. I could only see his ass sticking up in the empty air. Then at last he reemerged with a frozen pizza box in his right hand and waved it at me. "That's dinner!" But I wasn't excited about a meal of this type. He sensed my lack of enthusiasm which suspended his arm in the air for a while as if he'd forgotten it in the neon light. He looked back into the dumpster and said: "Here as well I buried my pride," then climbed down. In his living room, we shared the pizza after heating it in the oven. He said he had no money for rent and the landlord had threatened to evict him. Bari would leave his place by month's end, which was in a few days, and be back on the streets. I understood the secret of his sorrow and asked him: "What will you do?"

—I'll become homeless.

—Come stay with me in the studio, stay for free.

—No, man, enjoy your solitude.

—And you?

—I need to return to my past as a beggar.

—You need to?

—Yes, yes, I will test people's limits in good deeds.

I felt as if he was waiting for me to lend him a hand, but I had no money: "Forget about it and move in with me," I said.

—No, man, enjoy your solitude. I might get a job.

I felt a profound heartache. He adored the distance between us. I said: "I'm going home. Do you want Don to come with me or to spend the night at your place?"

He laughed: "No, man, take him with you, take him, we're too much for each other."

And he did get a job. At McDonald's. He was jobless for years, living on church charity or I have no idea what, I simply didn't know. Half an hour into his new job, he quit and came to see me at 8:30 a.m. at the Last Exit.

—Why did you quit?

—Man, as soon as I walked through the door, I saw a large hall packed with tables, and on each table the chairs were flipped, and on each chair there was a Bari sitting, and then all of them shouted at me when they saw the broom in my hand and said: By God, sweep the whole area, all of it, come on! So I told them I wasn't going to clean a thing before they all came down from their thrones. They said: We won't come down before you clean the whole area. And that's how they did me, man, can you imagine?

Bari was narrating his reincarnation in pain, almost in tears.

—Don't expect everyone to be kind with you, Bari.

—Dharmakirti said that the right action should always be preceded by the correct knowledge of things. And those folks are ignorant.

And he became homeless. I rarely saw him after that. Now and again he'd stop by to see me in the morning at Last Exit. He never spoke of his homelessness. His clothes were always clean, as if he'd washed them in public laundromats. And his Marines jacket was stuffed with crumpled computer paper on which he'd write his thoughts in pencil. Not once did he complain or explain what was going on with him. Not once did he appear unnerved or out of sorts. He said that his survival on the streets depended on two sentences: "Remain alone," and "Maintain your worth within yourself."

In the heart of every homeless person like Bari there are two people: a beggar and an emperor. When he was digging in a dumpster for a frozen pizza, his emperor was weeping. Still, Bari never lost his golden sense of laughter.

One time he told me as he was cracking up: "I will publish a newspaper called Bari Daily. I've even written the editor's announcement. I'd want to hear it if I were you."

Off a computer paper he started reading and giggling: "Lately I've noticed that my news doesn't reach you. No paper publishes it every morning. I am delighted to inform you that Bari Daily is here. You will now know my news first hand. And I promise you, on my honor, that the contents of the paper will not be as dull as the editor's word."

The idea made me laugh. I asked him how he passed the time in the world of the margins. He said: "I am busy building a small spaceship for one passenger and I will use it for travel when my time on Earth is up. I'll head to the stars in deep space and won't return."

—But until then where will you sleep?

—I'm bored with the well-lit mansions.

—What mansions?

—Those by the shore.

In summary, he was bored with seeing those lit mansions by the ocean during his homeless nights. Each one had a "private property" sign on its gate. Each night he imagined he owned one of those mansions, lived in it by himself and then, bored again on the next night, he'd move into the neighboring mansion. And so on until he concluded the list. He was eager to describe to me the shower curtains of each place, the bathroom robes, the masks on the walls. Private property limits the imagination. Sometimes we imagine ourselves in a house that is not ours, more extravagant than ours. Bari's imagination is greater than any border. I took this to heart: a wide imagination in a narrow world is necessary.

He said he was going to "become a billionaire one day." "How?" "I will go down to Berkeley, study clinical psychology, open up a practice, be the greatest soul doctor on the planet, and I'll become a billionaire. You know what, Hussein? There are people who possess no thought, they stroll in supermarkets shopping for thoughts. This is intellectual consumerism. And my mind is pure gold, a gold mine for the soul, ever new, doesn't shop, pure gold, man."

—And what is your mind's gold?

—Understanding. No matter what happens, it is under-standing. I won't tire of repeating that one word to you: understand, understand, understand.

—And what is understanding.

—Understanding is to understand what understanding is, and what it can do.

—And since I don't understand now what understanding is or what it can understand, does that make me stupid?

—Yes, yes (he burst out laughing). I love how your mind works.

—Why should I understand?

—There's a pleasure in contemplating people's issues. Understand, understand, and distinguish, distinguish. That's the summary I leave you with: understand and distinguish.

And he returned to his homelessness. I saw less and less of him. It was spring and I needed a lot of rest and a lot of sleep. I needed to see the ocean, the sun, to resemble Ali Baba when the cave door opened to the outside. I needed an ordinary space. How remarkable it is when the ordinary becomes an ambition. I used to dream of an ordinary sky, of good sleep over green grass under the sun near the ocean, of dozing off in a tree's shade on campus, of watching a gray squirrel leap from one shadow to the next, then stand on its hind legs and stare at me.

Seattle is beautiful in spring: the ocean blue, the snow-capped Mount Rainier, that deceptive mountain. Thinking it was an hour or two away, I started walking toward it one day, and after hours of walking, the mountain looked unmoved, not an inch closer. I hailed down a motor biker, asked him how far the mountain was. He laughed: "Maybe two hours by car." I grew up with short mountains. Mountains like Rainier were outside my realm of knowledge. As were those black and blue motionless clouds in the horizon, they perplexed me. For months I contemplated their stillness before I was told they were not clouds but mountain peaks.

I ran into Don one morning. Pure coincidence. I hadn't seen him since pizza night with Bari. "Hello, Don, how are you?" He let out a soft chuckle, rolled his red beard on his chest, and as he shook my hand, said, "I was in jail."

—Jail? Why?

—I collected my trash, my empty soda cans, paper piles, sticks and branches, and spread them in front of Safeway, so they called the police to arrest me for vandalism.

—And why were you trying to set up shop on the grounds of another seller?

—I can't leave the field open for monopoly. I introduced competition.

We laughed, walked to a museum on campus. "How is Suzan?" "Good, Suzan is good," he said, "she told me that Bari and I place her on a pedestal and worship her like Mother Earth and forget that she is an ordinary woman in need of a friend."

In the museum, we passed by a hard, solid, smooth rock. Not even five men like Don or I could make it budge. "Imagine," said Don, "an Indigenous warrior carried this rock for miles. They were real warriors. One tribe had a training exercise in which a person must run for miles in the sun with one sip of water in his mouth that he neither swallows nor spits out. Two battalions of the US Army hunted down two such warriors for months. They caught them eventually. I have a photo of them."

And I remembered Lewis, a homeless Indigenous man who sketched native faces to sell for a couple of bucks. I met him at that electric-toy store. The next day I called to him, "Lewis, Lewis," but he didn't reply. He changed his name to John. No force in the world could make him recognize me or "Lewis" whoever he was. On the third day, he changed his name to Johnnie and denied he'd ever met me, Lewis, or John. Whoever he was, Lewis, John, or Johnnie, he belonged only to his mutable name.

Don and I became vagabond partners for a while. He took me to each and every nook and cranny the young might have left their mark on. He took me to an airplane wing planted into the roof of a destroyed house. He showed me street art. But the most valuable thing he taught me in those days was how to read wood. He used to stare at the wood of cafe tables for hours, daydream while touching the wood, caressing its grain and lines, mumbling in astonishment, "No one paints what's in a piece of wood."

Then one day laughing Bari reemerged at Last Exit, said he'd solved his situation and was back at his old room. Our friendship resumed under a lot of tension until one night lightning struck me, and it became the saddest night in my life.

It was 1 a.m. We were at Bari's house. Joe and that drug addict, who saw naked women parading before him some nights ago, were with us. I was deep in a discussion with Joe, I don't recall what about. Bari was smoking, listening. I was tense, exhausted, everything in me disturbed, every belief, and every weakness spread like an oil spill in the water pond of a moonlit heart. In short, I was on edge, mentally and physically. Suddenly Bari entered the conversation: "Hey, man!" A bit perplexed, I stopped, waited for what he was going to say. "Your I is bigger than the city of Seattle," he said. I was stunned. The discussion was not about me, probably not about anything. A bout of madness swelled in me, and I extended my body like a bridge across the table and shook my finger in his face: "My I is bigger than New York, and I love it. Understood? Don't dare interrupt me again." Usually this would have been a moment we'd explode in, but this time my threat had a tone devoid of friendship, and I didn't think that this simple incident would bring about the downfall of our entire amity.

Astonished, Bari threw himself back into his wooden chair and silently rolled another cigarette. All his facial expressions changed in a manner I had not seen before. His face seemed to me like one of those paintings with phosphorescent green explosions that I'd seen in his room. His face became a cut-out square from a black and white photo, and out of that face green masses and waves emanated. He almost disappeared in the overflow. The light in the living room was yellow, the silence total. I realized something between us had broken: "Bari, I'm sorry, man, I really am."

He didn't reply, finished rolling his cigarette while staring at his fingertips. Joe and his friend got up and left. Bari and I remained alone. Time lapsed into eternity. Then Bari stood up and said: "Man, from now on you will not know me!"

He walked to an old guitar against the wall, opposite the kitchen door, a guitar I'd forgotten was there, and he grabbed it, sat in a chair away from me, at the far end of the table, bent over his guitar and started improvising a tune. I looked at him to try and detect his distant hideouts, but all I could see from his posture was Picasso's blue guitarist.

Before that night I'd not heard Bari improvise music like that. Maybe once at the pub in the university hotel, an underground pub with an old stairway in a narrow alley with dense smoke, pool tables, drunks, university students, and noise. There, he sat at the piano in the corner facing the wall and started playing. In one minute, everyone in the pub fell quiet. Those with glasses in their hands put them down. Those who were chattering shut their mouths. Everyone looked toward the corner where that hobo was playing and smoking, occasionally resting his cigarette on one of the keys. We were all invisible to him. His body swayed and swung to the tune that carried in it the same mad and magical ripples in the sea of his voice, the same lunar spume that rises out of deep black waves, the same metaphysical sorrow in his green painting, the same steep valleys in whose presence I'd always felt that no matter how much I knew him I'll never get to know him at all.

In that pub, it was the first time I'd known he was a musician. To him, my face was always a shore. On that night in his room, he was improvising on the guitar and singing:

Oh Lord, there's nothing you can't do,
and this means that what I can do is nothing.
Oh Lord, you know what's inside every heart
and this means I know nothing.

All I did was listen. As I listened, I fell and fell like a falcon's feather in dark wind and rain, fell into the immensity of a bottomless heart. I looked at him and found him crying, crying, snot running down his nose. He got up, wiped his tears and snot with the sleeve of his Marines jacket. I couldn't take it any more. I stood up and said "Bari, it seems the time for farewell is here." He nodded, yes. Mute minutes followed. I understood that I needed to leave. And in sadness I said: "Bari, bear with me one last time, one last question: If one day I write about all this, do I have your permission? If you don't give it, and that's your right, I promise you as God is my witness that I will not say one word to a single soul on this planet, not about you or about us."

He said "Forget Bari, man. It's best for you and for me not to write a word about it. But if you want to write, that's your call." He extended his arm and I extended mine.

I felt suffocated as never before, and walked out, down the wooden stairs to the street, looked back and saw nothing, he had shut the glass door, and a hand of the unknown grabbed my throat with fingers of tears and steel. I couldn't sleep that night and decided to catch him at Last Exit for his morning coffee as usual. But I dozed off and woke up at daybreak in a panic, the sun was out behind my glass wall, I ran to the cafe, it was open, there was no one there, so I sat by the glass window waiting and staring at grass and sun until a waitress in a white apron and caulked lips came and wiped my table clean, then paused, hesitated, and said: "Excuse me, sir, are you Hussein?" "Yes!" "A friend of yours called Bari came by earlier and wished you well. He left Seattle." "He left? When?" "An hour ago." "What did he look like?" "He had a wild walking stick and an old guitar." I choked, could barely speak: "Did he say where he was going?" "California. Santa Monica. He won't be coming back."

I left the cafe in absolute misery. I never saw Bari again. I felt a cosmic emptiness on an earth that closed up on me. I felt that every place was a ruse. In vain, I tried to forget. His face kept jumping out at me from every nook and cranny. Aimlessly I wandered as my mind leapt from one memory we had shared to another.

In the Eighties, I was enrolled in a philosophy course with that American professor who was mesmerized by Ramallah's empty night streets under yellow lights, and I was preoccupied with questions on the nature of madness. Somehow, we drifted into a discussion about the Old Testament wherein God tells Moses to get the Israelites out of Egypt, and Moses asks God: "And who shall I say sent me to them?" God replies: "I am that I am," that's who. In Hebrew, the sentence means: I was who I was, I am who I am, I will be who I will be. The professor lifted his gaze above his white eyeglasses that hung on his nose to look at me: "Hussein, what does God's reply mean to you?" I said: "Let's assume the God is an iris, and I know nothing about irises. I ask the iris, who are you? She says: I was an iris, and am now an iris, and will be in future time an iris. Now I wouldn't necessarily understand from her reply but one thing, that the iris is an eternal iris, and yet I know nothing about any iris or the meaning of all this." The professor nodded.

To me, madness was like God, this kind of iris, the kind I know exists, and was what it was, is what it is, and will be what it will be. I was ignorant about it, save only its "existence."

But it occurs to me that I asked Bari about this once: "What is 'I am that I am'?"

He said: "Wow, man, wow, that is the blue light!"

His reply startled me. I'd heard him speak of "the blue light" a few times. The first time, he said that my "blue bird" had visited him at night. The second time, he said he'd return the blue light to its home naked. The third time, we were walking through small trails in the woods on campus back to his apartment, and we reached a low cement wall in neon light. He mumbled to himself: "No, no, Bari, I said, no, Bari." I asked him what he was forbidding himself from, and he did not reply. Then later he spoke: "In every person there's a mysterious force ready to copulate with father, mother, tree, and monkey."

Maybe he saw himself sleeping with any of those in his mind and felt he was committing a forbidden act? Cynically I said, "Morals are petrified compulsions, don't listen to moral hymns." He said, "Man, enjoy your life. I have my private hell." I said, "Maybe, but breaking with forbidden morals may lead to such a hell." He got angry. I couldn't tell why. He said, "If you look at this world through the eyes of the blue light, you'll see that there are no morals, and there never were any." I said, "How do you distinguish between good and evil when you're in the company of the blue light?" He said, "Through taste. I don't do anything that I have no taste for." I tiptoed around his position toward sex and the blue light, "Were you ever a woman in a previous life?" "Yes, I was," he said, "and then it got boring. I used to go crazy whenever I saw a penis.

And creatures would descend from my butthole and chant at me: Queer, queer, queer!"

—Was that of your taste?

—And of the blue shadows.

Out of similar fragments, I gathered what he meant by the blue light. I went on searching in the library of secrets, in worlds I'd not heard of before, or that anyone besides Bari had heard of, that is, if he had heard of them at all. This is what I've been trying to write down and find difficult to approximate and bring forth. I can't narrate what the blue light was for Bari because he spoke in charms and spells. One night, after some of the usual beating around the bush, he spoke in a suggestive nondeclarative manner about Moses's journey in Egypt: "When the blue light went to Egypt, his scales fell off."

—Tell me in simple words, what is the blue light?

—You'll reach it through one of two ways: dancing or mind.

—And reaching it, is it like climbing stairs?

—Yes, pass yourself on the way, which you can do through being or through concepts.

—How do I pass myself through being?

—When you explode like a blue energy in the universe and you return the blue light naked to its home.

—Through dancing, for example?

—Yes.

—And how do I reach it through concepts?

—Through language that overflows me onto you, and overflows you onto me, until you learn to overflow yourself onto yourself.

—And if I reach it, what will you call me?

—The total mind.

And he said that latter expression in Arabic, which surprised me, as if he was referring to al-Farabi's concept.

That's how he often talked. It's futile to deliver his words to someone who can't capture their meaning with the knowhow of oracle or jinn. Or am I supposed to be "more precise" here? A French artist once said that precision is not the truth. And I say, don't ask precision or chronology of me, because time is for those who possess organized knowledge of when a thing occurred. I just don't know. I contemplate my memory as a sequence of events, and to each sequence a file preserved in memory, true, but the heart has a different order of things, a different arrangement. Something that happened twenty years ago appears to me as if it happened yesterday. And what happened two years ago appears as if it happened twenty years before. The heart rearranges its furniture according to the importance of events as the heart deems it. The heart couldn't care less about the system of dominant time or the system that time should dominate. And precision, as far as my experience with Bari is concerned, will lead only to nonsense. Who, for example, wants to accurately transfer how sea waves collide under the moonlight, or what the blue light is?

Fady, my brother, asked me as I was composing this book: "What connects a rabbit of a Shia fortuneteller woman in Beirut to a rabbit in the mind of a megalomaniac in Amman to the rabbit of a Sufi in Seattle to the rabbit in the text you're now writing?"

"You can call what binds all these things together, the blue light," I said.

In any case, I am aware that the blue light is a mysterious feel. And in travelling toward it I should not lose my normal usual senses of what is around me. To achieve this, I came up with a useful technique: to mute my distances from those around me by wearing a mask I call "the ordinary," whenever I can. This way I'd resemble a circle's center: my circumference touches the outside air, but my circumference remains closed on my center in the depths of an ocean as an embryo is in its mother's womb. And that depth, that womb, that "battn" is a mask. Would you please give me? Give you what? Another mask, a second mask. That's what Nietzsche said.

I made up my mind to retire several of my habits: to not seek being first or, as Goethe said, to build my house on the void, and that's why the whole universe is mine. Some people might call this vagrancy or queerness. They'd be paying attention to all that is external, to all my outside layers, my scales, and I'd have to fortify my mask with longer hair and weird sandals, whatever that might serve as another layer of scales to distance people from my center and my soul: my wardrobe, hair, homelessness, vulgarity. People will think what they will, so be it. That's useful to me, a third mask. Give me. Give me what? A third mask, please, yet another.

And I must not wrestle with people in their worlds. I will retreat into my spiral shell of a handful of relationships with "exceptional" folks only, as few as possible, and transform, as I learned from *Way of the Peaceful Warrior*, from an exceptional person in an ordinary world to an ordinary person in an exceptional world. I will choose my battles, avoid the futile ones, and let my avoidance be that of a ghost who leaves his house always after midnight, to walk in back alleys surrounded by well-lit villas, cocktail parties, lousy music, sex, politics, vying for positions, and howling. All I want is that no one notices me passing by. Please, give me. What? Another mask, a fourth one.

I will pile mask after mask on my face. Under all of those masks I will ascend naked to the blue light, naked and alone. And from a distance I will know in my heart for sure that other birds are headed to the same ascension, birds that I will greet from afar as I kill every sorrow inside me that breaks my soul and complains of the journey's loneliness, and I will dance. Give me, please. What? Another mask, a sixth mask.

"Mask song?" I felt I understood at last the famous story of Mohammad as he fled Quraish in Mecca to a cave in a nearby mountain. The trackers passed by the cave, saw a spiderweb, and thought "No one's in there." The Prophet's mask was a spiderweb. No one was there. God concealed his Prophet's face with a spiderweb, a mask, and the people of Quraish couldn't fathom that behind the web was a human face. This is the best kind of mask: the face appears to the outside world as a spiderweb, and no one can see through it except those who have travelled in the company of the blue light. Mohammad meditated in his cave. Meditation was his transcendent devotion. But they distorted it and said, "He worshipped in his cave." They distorted it to open a path for the ignorant who don't contemplate, who have proliferated to the detriment of Arabic and Islamic culture—which is what drove one of that culture's highest minds, the Great Sheikh Muhyiddin Ibn Arabi, to lament the abundance of "believers" during his age and the paucity of "knowers, possessors of kashf," that mystic revelation. Still, no, I don't mean anything by this, I take back my words, please, give me. What? A mask, a seventh mask.